P.S. Tell No One

Vikki VanSickle

with cover and original illustrations
by Holly Allerellie

Scholastic Canada Ltd.

Toronto New York London Auckland Sydney
Mexico City New Delhi Hong Kong Buenos Aires

For anyone who has ever had a question,
but wasn't sure who to ask.

Scholastic Canada Ltd.
604 King Street West, Toronto, Ontario M5V IEI, Canada

Scholastic Inc.
557 Broadway, New York, NY 10012, USA

Scholastic Australia Pty Limited
PO Box 579, Gosford, NSW 2250, Australia

Scholastic New Zealand Limited
Private Bag 94407, Botany, Manukau 2163, New Zealand

Scholastic Children's Books
Euston House, 24 Eversholt Street, London NW1 IDB, UK

www.scholastic.ca

Library and Archives Canada Cataloguing in Publication
Title: P.S. tell no one / Vikki VanSickle ; cover and illustrations
by Holly Allerellie.
Names: VanSickle, Vikki, 1982– author. I Allerellie, Holly, illustrator.
Identifiers: Canadiana 20220424543 I ISBN 9781443194013 (softcover)
Subjects: LCGFT: Novels.
Classification: LCC PS8643.A59 P7 2023 I DDC jC813/.6–dc23

6 5 4 3 2 1   Printed in Canada 114   23 24 25 26 27

MIX
Paper from
responsible sources
FSC® C016245

THIS BOOK BELONGS TO

♡Sunny

(mp)

xxTwix

*HOOPS

KEEP OUT

Sept 14

I HATE MR. M! How can he take our phones away? Isn't that illegal? Or some kind of security issue? MP, you're the super genius, is that even allowed?

Anyway, joke's on him! I found this old diary at home and I brought it so we can write to each other and pass it back and forth. Plus this way it looks like we're actually working. This might be my best idea ever? Smartest kid in the class 4 SURE! ☺

♡Sunny

P.S. Tell no one! And don't use any real names!

I think we all know who the smartest kid in class is (I'M TALKING 'BOUT YOU, MP). But even I have to admit, this is brilliant, Sunny! I love the whole diary thing! We're so old school, like Anne Frank. Years from now people will find this relic and marvel at our young, brilliant minds. 😉

xxTwix

OMG YOU CANNOT COMPARE US TO ANNE FRANK!!! Disrespectful much?? I cannot believe you said that. FTR, whoever reads this, I do not think I am IN ANY WAY like Anne Frank, who was a hero and victim of a horrific WAR CRIME. I am just an average kid who luvs music and Sloppy Jo — THE BEST DOG IN THE WORLD — and has never been kissed and probably never will be, but even then I know I am so fortunate to live here and not during WWII and I count my blessings every day. PEACE!

♡Sunny

Don't make me laugh in geography or else
Mr. M will know something is up! There
is definitely nothing funny about rock
formations, or Anne Frank, which you
obviously know, Twix. I swear, one of these
days you're going to make the wrong joke to
the wrong person and end up in the office
with Smelly Melly. Her perfume is so strong!
I had a coughing fit when I dropped off
attendance this morning. I'm pretty sure
the no-fragrance policy applies to all staff
including the secretaries, so maybe someone
should politely remind her?

I don't think it's TECHNICALLY illegal to
take our phones away. It feels like it's a
Mr. M-specific policy, not a school policy, so
you may have grounds to contest it.

Also, if we agree to do this, no one can find
the diary. I'm serious. Even without using our
real names, they can analyze our handwriting
or the people and situations we talk about
to figure out exactly who we are. If anyone
finds out and they call my parents I'll be
grounded for life! You'd never get to see

me and then you would have to live with yourselves, knowing you essentially signed the death warrant that killed my social life.

(MP)

Sept 15

Relax, MP! We'll be sneaky! Your perfect reputation will remain perfectly perfect and your parents will have no idea you pass notes in class, just like they have no idea that you listen to music with swears at lunchtime. 😉

Code names only! Also I think we need a code name for the diary in case we have to bring it up in public. Here are some ideas. Vote for your fave by placing a checkmark. My personal fave is PAD, but no pressure.

xxTwix

PLEASE ♡ ♡ ♡
VOTE!

- The Bible ← probably sacrilegious?

← Definitely sacrilegious!

- BOOK OF GIRL
(BOG FOR short)

BOG like
a swamp?!
Ewww gross

- GROUP DIARY ✓

- Pass-Around Diary ✓ ✓
(PAD FOR short) ✓

Like MAXI PAD kind
of pad? HAHA

PAD is actually kind of perfect, if you
think about it. If anyone overhears
us talking about it they'll be too
embarrassed to ask about it. Just imagine:

"Who has THE PAD?"

OK.
Ewwwwww!!!!!

"MP, can you give THE PAD to

Sunny when you're done with it?"

My vote is for PAD!

*HOOPS

P.S. I love EVERYTHING about this!

OMG that is so disgusting. haha I love it! UR A GENIUS! A disgusting genius! YAY! PAD! It's kind of fun to have a secret project. WAY better than this stupid goal project we have to hand in tomorrow! I don't know what to write down. Shouldn't a personal goal be just that? Personal? As in PRIVATE?? I hate that we have to get Mr. M AND our parents to sign it.

What happens if you don't achieve your goal, other than feeling like a complete loser? Mr. M can't fail you, right? What are all of your goals?

♡S

He ABSOLUTELY CANNOT fail you, it's just a personal growth exercise. There's no right or wrong way to grow! You should put down something easy. I put "read more." How can they argue with that? Reading is good for you! I don't have to say

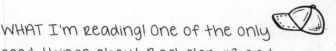

WHAT I'm reading! One of the only good things about Bachelor #3 and his daughters moving in this summer is that I now have an AMAZING selection of clothes and books.

xxT

You're probably going to have to be more specific than just "read more," Twix. We're not in grade six anymore. Mr. M is known for being kind of a tough teacher! Plus what if Mr. M makes you track your reading in a journal? Although I do love the idea of him looking up the titles online and finding a list of steamy teen romances!

I wouldn't worry too much about your goal, Sunny. Try not to think of it as something you're only doing for class, but a chance to do something you've always wanted to do. Speaking of which, I'm going to run for class rep. The Student Leadership team is something I've always wanted to do, even though the idea of running against Cheryl Blossom makes me feel sick and giving a speech in front of the whole class makes me feel even worse. What do you think, do I have a chance? Be honest!

(MP)

P.S. Don't tell anyone yet, it's still a secret!

OMG!

MP, that's AWESOME, you would be so great! Plus you only have to give a speech in front of our little class, not the whole school. It's just like giving a class presentation, only for something that actually means something to you.

YEAH!

My goal is to make the girls' basketball team. I practised a lot all summer and I did that basketball camp thing and I'm way better than I was last year. My secret goal is to make it to the county championships and get the winning basket, but I don't think that's the kind of "goal" Mr. M means. That's more of a dream, I guess. Is there a difference between a goal and a dream?

*HOOPS

Yes, dreams are fun and interesting and goals are BORING AND ENFORCED BY YOUR TEACHER. Why shouldn't you put down "win the championship"?

I think it's a great goal. UGH! You all have such great goals! And BTW, Twix, I DEFINITELY want to read your Fun Sister's sexy books! I LOVE that you have these two cool older sisters now. You can learn SO much from them (and then you have to put it in the PAD so we can all learn from their high school wisdom!).

I guess I'll put "don't fail math." But do you know what my actual, super-secret goal is? I want to be kissed this year. Obviously, I can't put that on the form. I feel stupid even admitting that here.

♡S

P.S. TELL NO ONE! Srsly, I'll DIE if this gets out!

Now that is a REAL goal and something I can totally get behind. 😊 My secret goal is to kiss MORE people. Maybe I'll put THAT on the form. It would be worth it just to see Mr. M's face! Why should our goals only be about school things?

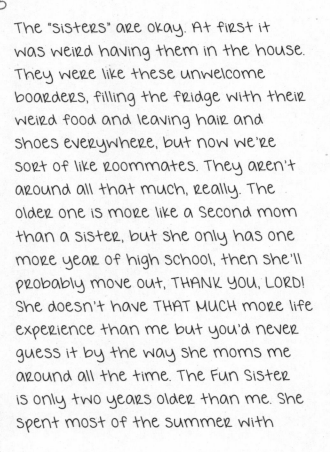

The "sisters" are okay. At first it was weird having them in the house. They were like these unwelcome boarders, filling the fridge with their weird food and leaving hair and shoes everywhere, but now we're sort of like roommates. They aren't around all that much, really. The older one is more like a second mom than a sister, but she only has one more year of high school, then she'll probably move out, THANK YOU, LORD! She doesn't have THAT MUCH more life experience than me but you'd never guess it by the way she moms me around all the time. The Fun Sister is only two years older than me. She spent most of the summer with

her new girlfriend, so I didn't see
her much. But they just broke up so
she's moping around a bit more.

XXT

Sept 16

I WISH I had older sisters or stepsisters
or roommates or whatever you call them.
I'd trade them for my younger brother
any day. He's totally out of control and
my parents don't even care, or worse,
they think it's CUTE! Like this morning
he kept smirking and calling me Rudolph
because of the big zit at the end of my
nose and my parents laughed like it was SO
CLEVER! Don't they see they are raising
a mini psychopath? MP, you've met him, he's
definitely on the way to murderville, right?!

♡S

P.S. Tell the truth, how bad is it? I knew
it was coming, I could feel it hiding there,
under the skin, like PULSING, like this
huge evil zombie zit! 😖

I hate to break it to you Sunny, but your brother is just a regular-level of annoying, at least by my own experience. It'll get better as he gets older, though. Now that he's in high school, my brother is much too cool and too busy to notice me most of the time, but at least he isn't burping in my face anymore. It is our job as sisters to know when to put up with it and when to shut it down. No one said it would be an easy task, but with great power comes great responsibility, or so some would say.

(MP)

P.S. Rudolph was totally uncalled for and very inaccurate. You can hardly see the so-called "zombie zit" and I'm not just saying that. The school pictures aren't really close-up and I think they use some kind of filter anyway.

Sometimes I imagine what my life would be like with a brother or a sister, but honestly, I kind of like that it's just me and my mom. If you guys ever need a break, you can always come over to my place. It's pretty calm and quiet, if you don't count my mom interrogating your every single move. But she's at work a lot, so it's not too bad.

*H

P.S. If it makes you feel any better, I can't see the zombie zit from my desk so it's probably average, which means no one really notices it.

Thanks friend!

You're just saying that because you're my friend, which is sweet but not helpful. I know what it looks like. It's like someone stuck an ugly tomato seed at the end of my nose and then I had a major allergic reaction to it. Plus it's picture day, which means it will be immortalized forever and ever. No cute #TBT pics for me. Also there's a boy who takes violin right before my piano lesson and he is SO cute and SUCH a talented musician, but he barely acknowledges me when he comes out and I'm about to go in.

It's like five minutes of torture every Tuesday! Just my luck that today is the day he looks over and what does he see? Zombie zit! 😖

I don't get it, I use toner and moisturizer and all the things they tell you to use and I still have the worst skin in the whole class.

Maybe I'll skip pictures. There's a retake day, right?

♡S

ZOMBIE ZIT is here to ruin your day!

AND YOUR PICTURES!

yeah, but then you run the risk of having an even worse skin day on retake day. If you get them taken today and they're really bad, you can retake. That's what I would do. Also on a scale of 1 to 10, it's like maybe a 6.

XXT

P.S. Don't think we didn't notice you NOT talking about Violin Boy! SPILL IT!

Okay. I guess that's fine. What choice do I have? Seriously, though, all those face washes and acne creams should be sued for false advertising. I don't know what to say about Violin Boy, I barely know him. Maybe he's my first kiss? I'd probably have to talk to him first . . .

My mom says acne is hormonal and there's very little you can do. Look around, everyone has skin issues, and some people have it way worse than you do. I look like I have a rash on my forehead half the time! You worry way too much, Sunny!

*H

Well then they shouldn't tell you on the package that they can fix it! Wait . . . hormones, as in period hormones? Is bad skin the price I have to pay for my period to finally show up? PLEASE SAY YES!

♡S

Sept 17

I don't think they're called period hormones, but yeah. Speaking of periods, is everyone ready for sex ed? Coach mentioned it at the basketball tryouts. Some of the grade eights were talking about this ancient video they had to watch that was totally cringe. AW swears her older sister watched the same one when she was in grade seven, and that was ten years ago! I bet you an entire package of Sour Patch Kids they start with the same video.

Not me, my parents wrote a letter excusing me from that part of the curriculum. I guess you Padlings are going to have to be the ones to teach me the birds and the bees — scary thought! 😋

Wait, what?! If my mom writes a note, can I be excused from history, please? It's all a bunch of lies about old white dudes anyway. Seriously though, they can do that? That's crazy! Are you mad about it? I would be!

P.S. Why do they use the phrase "birds and the bees," anyway?

It wasn't a surprise. I was expecting it. My brother didn't go to sex ed either. They don't think it's something that should be taught at school. I'm not mad exactly. I just wish they could see that it's just a class, like any other. It doesn't mean my values are going to change or I'm going to run out and start doing it with the first boy I see! But my parents don't see it that way and you cannot argue with my parents when they've decided something!

Mostly I'm a little embarrassed. What if I'm the only person in our class who sits out? I know people already see me as this innocent teacher's-pet type. I'm okay with that, most of the time, but I want to be taken seriously. Especially if I'm going to be our class rep for the Student Leadership team!

We'll miss you MP, but don't worry. We'll record the **HIGHLIGHTS** of what happens here in the PAD so you can feel like you're really there, but it will be so much better because you won't have to hear Coach saying words like "ejaculate."

Now I am thinking about this. THANKS A LOT, HOOPS!!!! xo S

P.S. I never thought about the birds and the bees thing but, yes, that makes no sense at all! How would that even work, like, physically?

Okay it's the birds and the bees time. I need to put the PAD away so I can give puberty my **FULL ATTENTION.** We'll miss you, MP!

Sept 21

Okay so you didn't miss much, MP, just a big talk about being respectful in class (meaning don't laugh at each other) and a super lame movie. The actors were, like, THIRTY. I couldn't stop laughing. Actually, everyone was laughing. Coach was NOT IMPRESSED (cue the big talk about respect). You were so right, Hoops! I owe you some Sour Patch Kids.

P.S. You're gonna share them, right?

WHAT DID I TELL YOU? You all owe me your best, most sugar-filled premium snacks. Mom is really into this no refined sugar, no fat, no good diet thing and it just might kill me. I like green grapes just fine but they are not Fuzzy Peaches. But if I keep my candy stash at school, she'll never know!

You also missed a handout of the female reproductive system. Here, I'll draw it for you, MP. I know your life will not be the same without knowing exactly where your cervix is located.

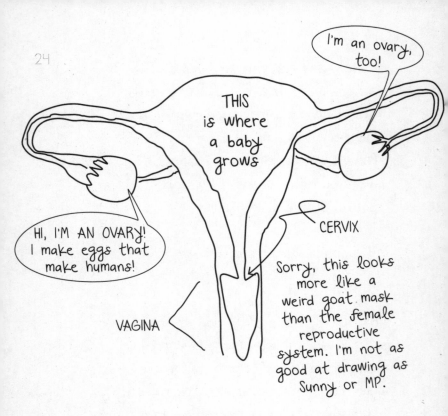

LOL I love it! Not bad, Hoops! Am I crazy or is cervix also a kind of cat?

You're thinking of a serval cat, not a cervix cat, Sunny. ☺

Thanks, Hoops. That's a pretty good drawing, only a little bit goat-like.

That movie is SERIOUSLY old. Based on the shoulder pads and all that weird bubble font, I'd say it's way before our time, like 90s maybe, but not the cool part! Why is everything in sex ed so old? Oh, well. At least I actually did the handout, that's a first! Also, call me weird but I really love the word fallopian. It's so pretty!

YOU DID NOT JUST SAY THAT!!!

HAHAHA! Fallopian is definitely better than testicle. Or mons pubis. What does that even mean? Is it French? Like, my pubis? That doesn't sound right . . .

It means pubic mound. It's Latin. I'm not even in sex ed and I know that.

Mound, like a pitcher's mound? I don't get it. No wonder people are weird about all things sex-related. The words are so bad! Except fallopian, the most beautiful word in the whole world! I'm going to write an ode to the fallopian tube.

Fallopian Forever
A poem by Twix

Fallopian is my favourite word.

It's the prettiest thing

I've ever heard.

Like a flower or a European state,

Fallopian sounds really great.

A swirling, curling muscle tube

So much cooler than my boobs.

Truly your BEST work!

SRSLY STOP! I'M DYING!

You've really made me look at fallopian tubes in a new way. A+

You should submit it to the poetry contest or maybe even the yearbook. Fallopian Forever needs to be immortalized as the work of genius that it is. Oh, and one more thing, Coach is putting a question box in the room. You can write a question on a slip of paper, put it in the box and she's going to read them aloud and then answer them. The whole thing is totally anonymous.

Well, except for the fact that it's right there out in the open, so ANYONE can see you put a question in. It's practically sitting on Bowtie's desk! He has a front row seat to the mysteries of the question box! Not that he would tell anyone, he's such a sweetie. And SO cute! Sigh! If only he was into girls.

And also, what if Coach recognizes our handwriting?

Disguise ideas for question box submissions

Why, DO YOU have a question you want answered, sweet little Sunny? Something about S-E-X? I wouldn't worry about it — it's not like we have a lot of handwritten work or assignments in gym. Coach probably has no idea what any of our handwriting looks like. Mr. M might know, but he's not the one reading them. THANK GOD! Can you imagine?

Sept 23

Before anyone ~~says~~ anything, I DID NOT put that question in the question box, so can we never mention it again? Okay, thanks.

It's just that nobody else in the class has red hair . . .

P.S. MP, for the record, this was the first question Coach read aloud from the box: If your hair is red, does that mean all of your body hair will be red?

Don't you think I would know the answer to that question? I swear on the junior girls' basketball championship that I did not put that question in the question box.

**** CONVERSATION OVER! ****

Oh no, Hoops! I can understand why you'd be upset about that. I would be, too! I can't believe they didn't separate the boys and girls this year. That must make things so awkward. At least I'm not the only one whose parents won't allow them to learn about "the birds and the bees." Grubby Thumbs and Mouse were in the library too. Mouse refused to do anything and played on their phone, and Grubby Thumbs chewed his fingernails the whole time. It was disgusting. I moved to another table, but I could still hear it. How often do you think they vacuum the floors in there?

P.S. Did you find out why it's called the birds and the bees yet?

I wish I was there with you, MP! I would rather sleep on the manky, unwashed library floors on everyone's crushed fingernails and shoe dirt for a whole year than have been in that stupid class. People kept looking back at me and smirking. I was so close to standing up and screaming in the middle of class THAT WAS NOT MY QUESTION! Maybe I still will. I'm so mad at Coach for reading it aloud. Didn't it occur to her that I would have to sit there while people were thinking about parts of my body that are none of their business?

Okay, okay, so it wasn't you! We believe you. But who is thinking about your body hair, Hoops? The NOT VISIBLE kind. Someone obviously likes you! The question is, who????

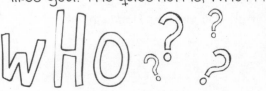

OMG I bet it's Swoosh! Remember how he came up to ask you about your summer on the first day? He did not ask any other girl that question. He literally left his group of guy friends and crossed the playground, just to talk TO YOU! It has to be him! You'd be such a cute couple! Sunnyside's top athletes, together forever. Are you into him?

Swoosh and I are just friends. And on the off chance that he did like me, and that's the reason he put that question in the box, that is the weirdest way to show it and I could never, ever go out with him. Swiftie is way more his type, anyway. She's, like, the star player. But I did make centre, so that's something. If only it wasn't ruined by the fact that everyone is thinking about the hair on my mons pubis (CRINGE!). This feels like too much humiliation for one person.

Dead from too much humiliation

Sept 24 ❀ ✳

Hoops, that is amazing. It's not even October and you're achieving your goals! You're a really excellent player, definitely the best player I know! You're the only girl my brother even lets play with him and his friends. Plus you have your secret goal to strive for! Maybe you were fated to be centre, and the magic combination of Swiftie as point guard and you as centre will carry the girls' team all the way to the county championship!

P.S. While I was in the library, I looked up the origins of the phrase "the birds and the bees," but I'm sorry to report it's not very clear. Most people attribute it to a few poets, but I read the poems online, and it feels like a leap to me. Definitely not very scientific, and not nearly as good as Fallopian Forever, Twix. xo

That's super nice of you, MP, but the centre is usually the tallest player, so I don't know that it's a glowing endorsement of my skills or just the fact that I'm (freakishly tall.) Being tall isn't exactly a skill so much as a fact. But maybe you're right, maybe we'll go all the way to the county championship. And Swiftie is a really good player, and probably my best friend on the team. I can't be mad at her. It just stings a little.

HEY! That's my friend you're talking about!!

You're an AWESOME basketball player and total goddess, Hoops, like the women who live on that island where Wonder Woman is from! And if Swoosh doesn't see that, that's his problem. (Although personally I still think he likes you). And I know you were totally and utterly humiliated, but the question did lead to something good! Coach talked about body hair and some hygiene stuff, which was very useful. Would you guys ever shave down there?

PARADISE Island!

Themyscira

OK, NERD! luv u!

MVP HOOPS!

P.S. Hoops, I know you don't want to talk about hair down there anymore, so obviously you don't have to answer if you don't want to. xoxox

Do you mean shave YOUR VAGINA? Use your words, Sunny. We, the Sisterhood of the Goat Mask, are young women who use PROPER names for things!

I think you mean VULVA. The VAGINA is on the inside. Remember the goat mask! Not everyone shaves. Coach said there are cultural or religious reasons to shave or not to shave. Do you think guys shave their pubic (cringe) area? Is that even a thing? Probably not. Nothing embarrassing happens to boys.

Oops! Vulva! I wouldn't shave everything, but the sides for sure. I wouldn't want anything showing at

the pool or something. My mom gets her bikini line waxed. It's supposed to last longer, but it's literally ripping hair out of your body, which seems like something that would hurt A LOT! My Fun Sister doesn't shave her pits or her legs, so I assume she also leaves her MONS PUBIS au naturel. I guess maybe I'm somewhere between them.

You never see a woman with any hair down there. Not that I'm an expert or anything, but in movies, or magazines and stuff, some of the things women wear are pretty revealing and it's not revealing any pubic (yuck!) hair. I hate the word pubic. Can we use something else? Maybe lady hair?

Pubic hair ISN'T restricted to ladies.

Okay, but what if you do decide to shave your VULVULAR area (happy now, Hoops?) and you accidentally cut yourself? I shaved my legs once, not that I needed to, I just wanted

PUBIC really is THE WORST word!

to try it out, and I pressed way too hard and ended up cutting my legs. It stung really badly, plus I had this horrible razor burn, like zombie zits, but all over my legs! I had to wear tights until it settled down so my mom didn't see and start screaming at me for shaving my legs too early. Not that I even had that much to shave. I can't imagine getting a razor in more SENSITIVE places.

Sept 25

New day, new topic! I wanna talk about how Swoosh was staring at our statuesque Basketball Goddess Hoops all through gym yesterday. Maybe it was the sight of your long legs in those sexy school gym shorts. 😉

Has he sent you any loooooooove notes yet? Cuz someone's got it baaaaaaad.

I totally saw that too! He's really cute, Hoops.
And polite and kind. IF you like him, I think
you'd make a good couple. But no pressure
if that's not what you want. Not everyone is
obsessed with romance.

Well I am! You would be too if literally
no boy looked at you ever! I don't think
they even SEE me as a girl. Sigh. This math
lesson is never-ending. When did math
get so hard? Here's the only math I care
about right now:

Hoops + Swoosh = SLAM DUNK

Enough! You'll just make it weird and
nothing, I mean nothing, can jeopardize the
basketball season this year. It's my goal,
remember? Do you want to be responsible
for ruining my goals?! Please just leave it
for now

→ FOR NOW?! SO you DO like
him! I knew it! Do you want
me to ask Dimples if he's
into you?

P.S. I hate those shorts. Why do they only come in two lengths, small child and enormous man? And why are our school colours mouldy yellow and rusty brown?

Technically it's mustard and maroon.

Technically IT'S UGLY! POOR HOOPS!

Wait, wait, are you with Dimples again? The very same Dimples who ditched you at the movie theatre last year and then the very next week was seen there with someone else? I thought we agreed to hate him forever and ever! Remember we did that curse thing and you burned the bday card he gave you? THAT Dimples?! Did I miss something?

OMG don't remind me of that night. That was SO dramatic! We're not together or anything, but we still text sometimes. And he's been commenting on all my posts lately. He was going through a lot last year and he actually apologized about the movie theatre thing. He felt really bad about it. People make mistakes, you know? I don't think we're over-over. There's still something there.

Plus until someone more interesting comes along, he's the guy I'm into now. There has to be someone to think about all day! Who do the rest of you have crushes on? I know about Sunny & Violin Boy, Hoops and Swoosh (DON'T DENY IT). MP? Anyone out there good enough for our future SL rep? There are lots of cute nerds for you to pick from at this school!

Sept 28

I know you think I have these crazy high standards, but that's not it. I just don't think about anybody that way. And I don't believe that everyone has to have a crush at all times. I certainly don't. Anyway there's SO MUCH to worry about, I can't imagine also worrying about boys too!

All I can think about right now is the speeches tomorrow. I really want to do Student Leadership but I hate public speaking (I think you know why). I've been dreaming about it since I handed in the application and I wake up with my stomach in knots and sometimes it's even hard to breathe.

Did you hear me when Mr. M called on me in geography just now? Just thinking about the speeches has made my stutter worse. It's like all that speech therapy was for nothing! And okay, I wasn't going to tell you all this, but today, at my locker, Cheryl Blossom walked right by me and said, "G-g-good luck t-t-tomorrow," smiling the whole time. Maybe I'm being too sensitive, but it really upset me. The speeches are only supposed to be two minutes, but what if I can't get through the whole speech before the two minutes is up? Do you think Mr. M will cut me off? That would be so embarrassing. Worse than losing to Cheryl Blossom.

P.S. TELL NO ONE!

WHAT A WITCHY B! 😠 MP, I know you worry about your stutter but literally no one cares. It doesn't mean you aren't smart or can't be a kick-ass class rep. This whole election is down to you and Cheryl Blossom (sorry, Bowtie!) and NO ONE REALLY LIKES CB! You're going to win and she knows it, so she's trying to freak you out. DON'T FALL FOR IT, MP!

Whoa, that is really low, even for her. I know how sensitive you are about your stutter but Twix is right, nobody cares and Cheryl Blossom is obviously threatened by you. You've known most of these kids for years, so they know about your stutter and I don't think anyone would be so low as to make fun of it or not vote for you because of it, except for Cheryl. Who, as we have said, is a terrible, horrible, no good, very bad person.

It's not like they laugh at you in class, right? Why would this be different? Plus your speech is awesome, which I know because I heard it when you practised last night. Seriously, it is like run-for-mayor-one-day, rule-the-world awesome. You're such a good writer and you are definitely going to win!

Truth!
↑
Agree!

THAT IS LIKE HUMAN RIGHTS VIOLATION LEVEL OF CRUEL! MP!!!!!! You're the nicest, sweetest, wouldn't say a bad thing about anyone EVER kind of person and everyone knows that. SRSLY I aspire to be as nice as you! The only reason Cheryl Blossom is popular is because she's so pretty and people are afraid of her, but the voting is anonymous, so people can actually vote for someone they like, LIKE YOU! I'm so mad she's attacking you like this.

P.S. I know you said tell no one, but isn't this bullying? The school goes on and on about zero tolerance. Isn't this exactly the kind of thing they're talking about? Obviously, you don't have to say anything if you don't want to, but I think this counts. And I don't think Mr. M would cut you off if you go a little long. He's a really nice teacher, even if he is from an entirely different century and says things like "the TikTok."

Thank you, Padlings. That means a lot. I know Cheryl Blossom is just being Cheryl Blossom, but it still hurts. I wish I cared less about my stutter, but when I get nervous it gets worse and then I feel totally helpless. I feel safer in writing — my words can be smooth and powerful and there's nothing to distract people from the message.

Why does public speaking have anything to do with being a good Student Leadership rep? Why can't we just hand out our speeches and have people read them?

That's a really good idea, actually, and when you get on the SL committee — WHICH YOU WILL — maybe you can change it. I bet other people would apply if they didn't have to give a speech. YOU CAN DO IT! XOXOXOX

Sept 29
ELECTION DAY
OTHERWISE KNOWN AS THE DAY
MP KICKS SERIOUS BUTT
(ESPECIALLY CHERYL BLOSSOM'S BUTT)

WE LUV YOU, MP!
YOU CAN DO THIS!

You can **DEFINITELY** do this!

What she said x 100. I'm passing the PAD to MP next so the last thing she sees before her kick-ass speech is our messages of love.

I DID IT! IT'S DONE! I can't believe it, but I actually feel good about it! I did what you told me to do, Hoops. I focused on it one sentence at a time and I put little stars on my paper so I knew when to look up. Each time, I saw your smiling faces and double thumbs up (Sunny, you're the very best) and it was okay! Thank you SO much, my dearest Padlings. I couldn't have done it without you or your kind words.

MP, YOU WERE AWESOME! You are definitely going to win. Even if I didn't know you and love you and I was just voting based on the speeches, you'd be my pick. Hoops was so right, that was an epically good speech! And before you say anything, I'm NOT just saying that because you're my friend.

Honestly, MP, I was so proud of you I got a little teary, like I was your mom or something! You were really, really

great and you're going to be our student
leadership rep, I know it. xo

She really did get teary, it was
adorable. You were rad. You're for
sure going to win. Cheryl was way too
smug, like she already had it. Plus she
barely talked about what she was
going to do! Like, what have you done
for ME lately, Cheryl Blossom? Other
than make me feel like crap about
those overalls I wore last week.
Which, BTW, were VERY cute and she
could never pull off, and she knows it!

I even think my stutter was okay. Not great,
but not the worst. I'm still a little shaky but
I think it's half leftover nerves and half relief.
It will be nice to have some time alone (or
mostly alone) in the library to calm down.

P.S. It's not exactly a free period, Twix.
Mr. M gave me an assignment to do. I have
to do a report on a discovery that changed

the medical and health industry. So far my research has been pretty disturbing. Did you know the CDC didn't create hand hygiene guidelines until the 1980s? Some people did it, but it wasn't common practice. I'm very, very glad we live in this century!

P.S. Mouse is STILL biting their nails. This may or may not have inspired my research.

Sept 30

The 1980s? We know people who were alive then! (Shudder!) Well, while you were watching Mouse devour their own hands, we were learning about periods, so even though we were separated, it's nice to know we all had a GROSS day. Yesterday's question was, Can you tell if someone has their period?

To be clear, some people knew about handwashing, it just wasn't ingrained in them like it is in all of us now. But still, gross! What sort of things did Coach say? Do you think a girl or a guy asked that question?

Most of it was pretty technical stuff, like what happens during the ovulation cycle, some stuff about cramps and PMS **(TOTALLY A REAL THING!)**. There wasn't too much giggling or anything. But I definitely think a girl asked that question. I doubt guys think about periods. Or if they do, they probably just think it's gross. They don't worry about it all the time like girls do. Or maybe that's just me who worries about it all the time.

Haha that's a laugh. Boys are gross. All that stuff about wet dreams? How is that LESS gross than periods? Thank goodness I will probably be out of the house by the time my brother the monster will be old enough to experience "nocturnal emissions."

P.S. Hoops, definitely not just you! I think about it all the time but I'm not so much worried as DYING FOR IT TO SHOW UP.

Is it just me or does
"nocturnal emissions" sound like
the name of a horror movie?

HAHA YES!

Agree!

AGREE!

Honestly, I think I'd rather have a
period than deal with a penis. At least
you can count the days and know when
your period is coming and you can deal
with it discreetly most of the time,
you know? Imagine waking up to discover
you'd had a "nocturnal emission!" Or
getting a spontaneous boner in class
or at a funeral or someplace totally
awkward! Guys can't control when they
get a boner.

Would you rather get caught with an
erection or a period stain in class?

WORST WYR question ever! I refuse
to answer! No to both!

WYR rules state that you must answer one or the other. NO SKIPS.

Does it count as a WYR if one of the options can't physically happen to you?

Obviously, the whole point of WYR is the most EXTREME, ridiculous scenarios ☺. MP, as our impartial judge and knower of rules, what's your verdict?

Objection overruled! This was a hard one, but I pick period. I really want to have kids someday and I love that my body can do that. I can put up with the cramps and the blood and everything that comes along with it.

If I HAVE to pick, then I guess I pick period too. But only because I have to, and FTR, I hate this WYR! Even though a lot of it sucks, I like being a girl most of the time. Plus I don't know how to deal with a penis. Okay this is embarrassing, but I've always wondered, how do boys ride bicycles? Isn't the penis in the way?

Rocky road?

P.S. DO NOT TELL ANYONE EVER!

LOL I can honestly say I've never thought about how boys ride bicycles, but now that I am thinking of it, I think it has to do with where the penis is located? On the diagram we got it's higher up than I thought, and when you ride a bicycle you sit on your butt, so I guess it's safely out of the way?

Even with The Bicycle Question, I would still pick erection over period stain. It would be so much easier to hide an erection than a blood stain. It's not like it's permanent or ruins your clothing. People would tease someone if they got an erection at school which is embarrassing,

Like, wouldn't there be BOUNCING?

OMG! LOLOLOL

but also sort of manly somehow? Nobody is proud of a period stain. If anyone caught you with a period stain you would never, ever live that down which is so weird because it's just blood! JJ had a nosebleed in gym and it was no big deal. It's such a double standard. See, these are the things I worry about! I don't know why you're so anxious to get your period, Sunny!

Sept 30

The double standard thing is so unfair but totally true. Can you imagine if boys got periods? It would be all they talked about. They'd probably brag about it and turn it into some sort of contest. Like, "Dude, my period was SO HEAVY today!"

The award for BEST STAIN goes to...

If boys got their periods they would definitely not be quiet about it. It would definitely be celebrated as something manly. It really makes you think. What are we so embarrassed about? If women everywhere decided to talk about their periods all the time, things would change. It's like that thing Coach is always saying, "Be the change you wish to see in the world." We should start a revolution! We can get Hoops' goat mask drawing printed on t-shirts and walk around the halls shouting:

FALLOPIAN FOREVER!

You know I love Fallopian Forever and I agree that change is necessary, and it would be nice to not feel so embarrassed about it all the time, but the truth is I'm not brave enough to just start dropping the P word into everyday conversation, and especially not with boys. It feels like something private, and I'm okay with that.

Maybe there's another, less public way I can help the revolution? Like organize your rallies? Help with posters?

P.S. Coach didn't make that quotation up. It's on a poster in the library. It's the first thing you see when you walk in.

I WANT A GOAT MASK T-SHIRT!
If I HAD my period I would totally join your revolution, Twix. But if I joined, I'd be a fraud, since I have exactly nothing to contribute. Maybe I could write music for Fallopian Forever and that could be the anthem? We could send it to Lizzo! Doesn't that totally sound like a song she would sing? Then we could all be millionaires and I'd never have to worry about math again.

Okay, if you had to pick one, which would you choose?

PICK ONE!

✔✔

OMG SO
GOOD!!

✔✔

OMG we
should sell
these!

You're not missing anything, Sunny, trust me.
Just a monthly mess and constant paranoia
that you had a leak or you're out of pads
and you'll have to ask someone for one. My
cramps are pretty bad too. I didn't get them
the first few times but now I get them all
the time. It feels like someone reached into
my stomach and is twisting everything inside
with their hands. At least it's only for the
first day. Seriously, enjoy your period-free
years while you can!

P.S. Both of those designs are excellent, but
I'm leaning toward the goat mask!

Hugs, MP! Your cramps sound so painful. I know it's not this FUN experience, it's just the principle of it all. It means you're a teenager, you're growing up, you're a WOMAN! At the very least you're not a little kid anymore. I hate missing out on things! The FOMO is intense, guys!

Happy second month of school!
One down, nine more to go!

OMG DON'T SAY THAT. NOOOOOO!!!!

I'm sorry about your cramps, MP. My mom gets them and she has this fuzzy hot water bottle she likes to curl up with. Maybe you could try that? Coach also said some people take medication, the kind of stuff you can get at the drugstore.

Cramp Care package

Um, I INTERRUPT THIS VERY
IMPORTANT DISCUSSION TO
CONGRATULATE THE NEWLY
ELECTED CLASS REP FOR 7B,
MP!!!!!! YOU DID IT!
I KNEW YOU WOULD!!! SO, SO
PROUD OF YOU MP, AKA MOST
PERFECT. XOXOXOX

I can't believe it! When Mr. M announced it and everyone started clapping, I smiled so hard my cheeks hurt. Am I still blushing? I feel like I'm still blushing! I don't know how I'm supposed to focus on anything else today! Thank you, thank you, thank you for all your advice! I couldn't have done it without you, Padlings!

Congrats, MP — aka MOST PROMISING! I KNEW YOU WOULD WIN! There was no way Cheryl Blossom was going to beat our MP. Speaking of, CB looks like she swallowed a big old bag of lemons today and I kind of love it. Serves her right. That's karma for what she said to you, and all the things she's said to all of us. You're going to be great! Not to mention that the VP is extremely dreamy. I can't believe you get to see him once a week. And that's just for meetings! You'll probably get to work together on projects or whatever you guys do on the SL team. Maybe there is a kiss in your future . . .

MP, YOU DID IT! My cheeks hurt from smiling too! I can't imagine how yours must feel. I'm so, so proud and happy for you!

P.S. Since Twix brought it up, I agree. VP might as well stand for VERY PRETTY.

Or Virtually Perfect!

You guys are too funny. But seriously, if VP stands for anything, it's **VERY** Professional, which is how we're going to keep things. I'm not interested in anything but official Student Leadership projects. Even if I was interested, he's friends with my brother, meaning not only does he have questionable taste in friends, but dating him would be like dating a brother, which is gross, not to mention totally wrong!

Whatever you say, MP, Queen of the SL committee! Okay, so I've been thinking about what Sunny was saying about what makes you a woman. You can be a woman and not have your period, remember? Gender is about how you feel inside and sex is about the biology stuff. So, like trans women don't have periods, but they are still <u>women</u>. —TOTALLY!

Good point!

YES!

Plus being a teenager literally just means you are between the ages of 13 and 19, which you are! I was at your thirteenth birthday party, remember? Personally, I am in no rush. It all seems like such a hassle.

Especially with sports. I know there are heavy-duty pads and tampons, but I still worry about it. Plus I don't think I could use tampons, at least not right away.

I used a tampon once! It was end of this summer. I was at a pool party at JJ's and I really wanted to go swimming with everyone. The hardest part was figuring out the right angle. It took me a while! I thought they would come looking for me to see if I had drowned in the toilet or passed out or something, but once I got the right angle it was easy to get in. I sort of pointed it up instead of straight in, if that makes any sense? It's hard to describe — you just have to do it! Once it was in, I didn't feel it at all. If you want to use them, I know you could all figure it out, you brilliant Padettes.

Tampons are great, but not so great for the environment, which, as you all know, is a big deal to me. My Fun Sister showed me her menstrual cup. Honestly, at first I thought it looked kinda big, but when you fold it up to get it in, it's way smaller. Then it pops into place and she swears you can't feel it. I haven't worked up the courage to try one yet, but I want to, eventually. In the meantime, she got me some reusable pads which are actually so soft and super luxe compared to the plastic disposable ones. It's like I'm treating myself on my period. Why shouldn't I feel like the queen that I am? You just rinse them out when you're done and then put them in the laundry. Super easy!

She showed you her menstrual cup? Gross! Obviously, I've never had to USE a tampon (sob!), but I took one of the tampons that Coach had at the front of the room so I could look at it on my own, privately. I didn't understand what she was saying about the applicator, so I wanted to practise pushing the applicator so I'd know what to do when my actual period shows up (HURRY UP, PERIOD HORMONES!). I get that part of it now, but then I put the tampon in a glass of water just to see how much it would expand and it got crazy big! I can't imagine putting one inside my BODY! I think it's going to be pads for me, at least until I'm older.

P.S. TELL NO ONE!!

LOL! YAH RIGHT!

If you don't, I will.

I dare you to do a science project comparing the absorption of tampons, Sunny.

OBVIOUSLY, it wasn't a dirty cup, Sunny! It's really easy to clean. She washes it out with soap and water and then when her period is done, she boils it in water. Plus how is using a cup different than wearing a tampon? One isn't grosser than the other. None of it is gross! That's just the patriarchy talking. It's natural!

My Fun Sister got me thinking about how totally messed up it is that we have to pay for period products. It's not like we choose to bleed, or when or how much. And in some places people still have to pay taxes for tampons and pads and stuff.

In her high school, sometimes they don't even restock the machine in the girls' bathroom. It literally ate their money and gave nothing in return, so these poor girls have to stuff their underwear with scratchy budget TP and then go back to class worried they might leak all over the chair! Isn't that awful? My Fun Sister thinks pads and tampons should be available for free in public washrooms, like soap and toilet paper, which totally makes sense to me! It's called menstrual equity. She wrote an article about it for her school paper. It's online somewhere, I'll send the link!

DOWN WITH THE PATRIARCHY! FALLOPIAN FOREVER!

Smart! *SO* smart!

P.S. <u>I always carry an emergency pad</u>, the disposable kind, in my backpack if you need one!

OMG SAME!

THIS! I had a literal nightmare about this!

That is my worst nightmare, getting it at school and having no way to deal with it. I wish there was some definite sign that it was going to happen, but Coach said there isn't. Most girls have some pubic (cringe) hair, but you could have it for ages before your period comes. Some girls have cramps, some don't (sorry, MP!). You just can't be 100% sure!

My mom told me about this magically

absorbing underwear you can just bleed into. She uses them and she already bought me a pair that is especially for "girls our age," whatever that means. But, like, do I wear those every day until my period comes, just in case?!

Oct 2

Okay, so I looked up those period underwear online last night and they are a real thing, but I still don't get it. They don't leak at all? How is that possible? And you just rinse them out and put them in the laundry like regular underwear? That's so easy!

Twix, I will bake you homemade Twix bars for a whole year if you get up right now and yell FALLOPIAN FOREVER. Actually, if you do decide to do it, can you wait until math? I am totally going to fail that stupid quiz today.

Science = magic, Sunny. They built spaceships to go to the moon, magical period underwear seems a lot easier. (And more useful! How many people get to go to space anyway?). Seriously though, what does "especially for girls our age" mean, Hoops? Do these period underwear have shiny rainbows and fluffy kittens on them?

P.S. I am seriously considering a large-scale class disruption. 😈

No kittens or rainbows, sorry. They look like normal purple underwear, but the crotch part is made of this special material designed to hold blood without leaking. I like the idea of period underwear better than pads or tampons. Once you've got them on, you don't have to think about getting up to change something every few hours. I guess I'm pretty lucky. Mom brings period stuff up all the time. It's no big deal, but at the same time it's a big deal to her. When it does happen, I'm worried she's going to invite her yoga class over to, like, welcome me to womanhood or something.

If she does, you HAVE to invite us. Please! I want to go to your Womaning party! When I got my period, Second Mom hid her tampons in "her" room (sorry, but up until very recently that was my actual mom's office) and told me to buy my own supply. Classic! My mom cried and poured herself a glass of wine. I think she was more upset by the idea that she was old enough to have a menstruating kid than choked up over her baby "becoming a woman." My Fun Sister took me for ice cream, though. Everyone should have ice cream when they get their period.

MUST PROTECT THE TAMPONS

Sunny, Hoops, I promise to take you for ice cream or whatever

you want when the Big Red Train
pulls into the station.

I definitely did not get ice cream. My mom
showed me where the pads were under the
sink and I got an uncomfortable five-minute
talk about responsibility, like I had turned into
a different person overnight. I had all these
questions but I could tell my mother was
embarrassed, so I didn't ask any of them. I
actually felt kind of sad, like something was
over and I could never go back. I wouldn't
describe it as a joyous moment in my life.

Aww, MP, don't think about it like
that. Why would you want to go
backwards, anyway? It's way more
fun to be a teenager than a kid. I'm
sure it was just those hormones
making you sad. Next time the Red
Menace shows up, I'll take you for ice
cream! Don't your parents know you
at all? You're the least likely person
I know to engage in anything fun, I
mean, scandalous. 😉

→ Roller coasters LOLOLOL
of **EMOTION!**
↑
NO!

Twix, promise me you'll never use phrases like the **BIG RED TRAIN** or the **RED MENACE** again. They sound like <u>roller coasters!</u> I still think that's crazy that your parents are keeping you out of sex ed, MP. It's not like Coach is telling us to go out and have all kinds of sex. It's just, like, anatomy and how babies are made and some safety stuff. Don't they think that's important? Can't you say something to them? Then maybe you can get some answers to your questions.

I could never! How am I supposed to bring up sex ed when my mom doesn't even want to talk about periods, which aren't even about sex, if you think about it. After that first conversation, she never brought it up again. All they will hear is the word "sex" coming out of my mouth and they'll completely freak out. It's fine, I'm getting much better info from you girls. Keep those questions and answers coming in!

Hey! I thought the Big Red Train was pretty good. WYR call your period the Big Red Train or Aunt Flo (like in olden times)?

YOU HAVE TO PICK ONE! 💩

Aunt Flo is so lame. What about something like Big Red?

That makes me think of my brother's favourite band, Big Red Machine.

Or Clifford the BIG RED Dog? GROSS!

KEEP CLIFFORD OUT OF THIS!

Poor Clifford! Okay, time to vote!

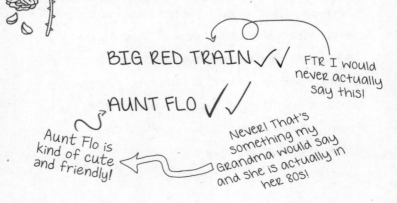

BIG RED TRAIN ✓✓   FTR I would never actually say this!

AUNT FLO ✓✓

Aunt Flo is kind of cute and friendly!

Never! That's something my Grandma would say and she is actually in her 80s!

Oct 5

I thought about what Twix said over the weekend, and I really love the idea of going out for ice cream the next time one of us has her period. It doesn't have to be ice cream, it can be anything. Whoever has their period gets to pick. It's like a solidarity thing. Everyone goes, even those of us without periods. (Okay, Sunny? YOU'RE A TEENAGER! You can come!) It wouldn't be like a "womaning" party (shudder!), more like a pick-me-up.

LOVE THIS!

I love this idea too! I'm telling you right now, when my period finally shows up I want a mochaccino ice cream cake, and maybe a party, but not a big one, just us Padettes! Maybe when we've all started, we'll sync up and get them at the same time. Isn't that a thing that can happen to women who hang out a lot?

My mom and the sisters get their periods around the same time and it's wild at our house. I'm not on their schedule yet, but then I only started a few months ago. It's been kind of inconsistent. My first period was three days, but then the next one was so light, like spotting, and I wasn't even sure if it was my period, but my Fun Sister says it will settle into a rhythm eventually. I found an app to track it. You can even put in your symptoms, like cramps or breakouts or whatever. We're probably all on Second Mom's schedule — she's so bossy it just makes sense that her uterus would boss other uteruses around. Is it uteruses or uteri?

Can you send me the app information? That sounds extremely useful.

P.S. When would you even need to use the plural of uterus?

I dunno, say you're a doctor and you're teaching new doctors and you want them to compare X-rays of many different uteruses/uteri? You're the genius!

Alright MP, today's question box question was: Can you get pregnant the first time you have sex?

Answer: Yes! It has to do with when you're ovulating. Fun fact: there is only a short window of time you can get pregnant, like three days. Gross fact: sperm can LIVE INSIDE YOU for five days! So even if you're not ovulating the day you had sex, you should add five days just in case. But obviously use protection, blah blah blah.

MATH! Even in sex ed, I can't get away. 😴 I failed the last quiz, which is obviously bad, but it's extra super bad because my parents said if I don't get a B in math, I can't do fun things, like go out with friends or to things like dances. I will literally be under house arrest!

Whoa, that's intense! I got a C, so I don't know how much help I would be, but no one ever asks to see my math quizzes so I don't have to worry that much. Do you think that was a hypothetical question, or is someone in this very class thinking about having sex? I just can't imagine anyone actually on the verge of having actual S-E-X.

That's a good quesetion. Do you think boys think about getting girls pregnant as much as we think about it?

I don't know. But I know I could never have sex without being in love.

Me too. I'm going to wait for marriage. I think sex is something sacred.

What if you don't get married? Does that mean you'll never have sex?

Why wouldn't I get married? It's a goal like any other, something you set out to accomplish. If you want to get married and have a family, you find the right person and you make it happen. I wouldn't sit around and wait for fate to figure it all out. Why would you leave something important to you up to chance?

That is so practical and so totally you, MP, but I just love the idea of fate. You know, star-crossed lovers and soulmates and all that. It's probably better to be practical about it, but I can't help it, I love the romance of it all! Love is, like, the closest thing we have to experiencing magic. I want to believe IN MAGIC!

Awwww... Sunny!

DEEP!

Oct 6

Okay, back to the sex thing, I would want to wait until I was ready and with someone I really liked, maybe high school or college? I can't imagine it now, but I can see myself being ready in like five or six years.

That seems like a long time. Aren't you curious? Plus I want to get my first time over with. People treat it like it's such a big deal, but if you're into it, and you're careful, why not? It's MY body, it's MY virginity! Plus once you do it, no one can use it against you. It takes the "is she or isn't she?" out of the equation.

But when you do it, and people know about it, they think you're a slut. You can't win. ☹ I'm more worried about what people would say about me than the actual sex part, which is kind of scary too (but way harder to imagine). How do you know if the other person will keep it a secret? Don't guys like to brag about sex? Even the nice ones will probably tell someone, and then that person tells another person and then before you know it, the whole world knows. Or at least the whole school, which might as well be the whole world.

But if you don't have sex, they call you a prude, so who cares what you do? It's like you said, you can't win, so follow your heart! LIVE YOUR TRUTH!

I think you're being a bit harsh. Maybe some guys do, but not all of them! And obviously I wouldn't be having sex with the kind of guy who would run out and tell everyone. Can you see *Swoosh* doing that? Or your brother, MP?

Does that mean you ARE having sexy thoughts about SWOOSH?

People only say "NO COMMENT" when they mean yes!

NO COMMENT.

WYR be known as a SLUT OR a PRUDE?

Prude (obviously). It's not even that insulting of a word, if you think about it. I'd rather be called a prude than stupid, evil, mean or a bully. And, honestly, I wouldn't care what a bunch of small-minded bullies with a two-point rating system for girls think. Their opinion has nothing to do with me or my values.

Plus I'm with Hoops — I don't believe every guy would look at the girls in his class and think, slut or prude? My brother, as irritating as he can be, would never do that. I don't think my cousins would, either.

P.S. Let's never mention my brother and sex in the same sentence again

SHE-RO

YOU'RE MY SHE-RO, MP! I wish I could be as confident as you. This is so hard. Prude, I guess? In a way, being a prude means you're sort of a romantic, like you're waiting for something special — in my case, Love-Magic. But if someone actually called me a prude to my face, or behind my back but then I found out about it, I'd be really embarrassed and would definitely cry about it later.

Me too. It's just so unfair that there are only two options and they are SO opposite. I don't know any prudes OR sluts, do you? I would choose slut, just for the principle of it. I'm with Twix — it's powerful in a weird way. Once they've called you a slut, what else can they do to you? YOU'RE FREE!

Oct 7

Okay, since none of us are having sex anytime soon, let's go back to kissing. Hoops, have you or have you not kissed Swoosh yet? Y/N?

Way to make me feel excluded. You know I haven't even had my first kiss yet. ☹

No comment. Twix, since you brought it up, how many people have YOU kissed?

What's with all the "no comment" garbage! The PAD is all about commenting! And since you must know, three and a half.

It is physically impossible to kiss half a person. Explain.

YES. PLEASE!

Three and a half!?!?! And I haven't even kissed ANYONE? No fair! Why is my life so TRAGIC AND EMPTY? Who are the lucky boys? The only one I know about is Dimples.

1/2

Okay, so it was half a kiss, not half a person, Miss Technical. The half kiss happened at camp. This guy Nahem missed my mouth and kissed my chin, which definitely doesn't count as an actual kiss. Therefore, it's more of a half kiss. It was also a little slobbery, kind of like when a dog gives you a big lick.

I KNOW THIS FEELING! Cringe!

Way to sell it!

So that leaves Dimples, obviously. We're definitely going to get back together at some point. Then there was JJ and don't get mad, Hoops, it was so long ago and it didn't really count, but number three was Swoosh. Before you

1

2

go all quiet and mad, it was a
dare and we didn't even open
our mouths so it barely counts.
I didn't say anything before
because it meant literally nothing
to me. Are we cool?

3

Ok, wow. I had no idea. I'm not mad, but a
little weirded out. And kind of shocked. You
don't hang out, like at all. When did this
happen, exactly? And were you planning on
telling me?

After the end-of-year party last
summer. A few of us were hanging
out by JJ's pool, playing truth or
dare, and it just happened. But it was
only once and we never talked about
it or even came close to kissing again.
He's all yours, I swear. We don't text
or anything.

Wait, is that why you left MP and me in the kitchen with JJ's mom and disappeared for, like, two hours? You went off to find some cooler people and ended up kissing Swoosh and you never even told me? That hurts!

I also did not know anything about this!

So it's not just me, then. Sounds like nobody knew anything about it. If it was no big deal then why did you keep it such a secret, Twix?

God I <u>KNEW</u> this would happen! You being upset about it just proves that you really like him, just admit it! I swear it didn't mean anything. Can we see this as a good thing and not like "Oh Twix is such a <u>slut</u>" thing?

Whoa, who said anything about being a slut? I'm just trying to process the very surprising news that you kissed the boy I like and **NEVER** told me. Even if it wasn't Swoosh, I thought we were the kind of friends who told each other this stuff.

Oct 8

Okay, I thought about this all night and I've decided to be totally honest with you, since the PAD is all about honesty. The tRuth is, I don't tell you guys everything because I don't want you to judge me. I see the way Hoops and MP look at each other when I talk about guys, like I'm boy crazy and therefore stupid or less serious than you or something. And, Sunny, you pretend to be all open-minded, but you can be pretty judgemental sometimes.

Maybe I don't want the three of you attacking me for being a **NORMAL**

person with normal feelings. It is
NORMAL to want to kiss people.
Actually, I think it's pretty abnormal
that out of the four of us I'm the
only one who has done any kissing.
I know I said I would pick slut over
prude, but that was just a WYR. That
doesn't mean I want my friends to
think of me as a slut. That actually
really sucks.

♡

Twix, I would never, ever call you a slut! You
know I hate that word! I'm sorry if I did
anything to make you think that. I would
never feel that way about you. I am totally
in awe of how mature you are! Sometimes
it feels like we're totally different ages. The
truth is, I'm a little scared of kissing and
everything else (I can't even think about the
everything else part)! I didn't mean to "look
at Hoops" like you say, and I promise not to
do it again. Can we please not fight??

♡ Love, MP ♡

OMG Twix, you are NOT a slut, don't ever say that! We just talked about how it wasn't cool to call anyone that! You're my hero! You are so chill around guys in a way I could never be. Three is not a big number at ALL. I just meant I was jealous that you had kissed three and a half boys! And I think you can totally have half a kiss, BTW.

Meanwhile I'm still wearing little girl undershirts and am practically invisible to boys. Seriously, YOU ARE NOT a slut and I think I speak for the entire PAD that none of us think that, and if we ever heard anyone calling you THAT WORD, we would set them straight.

I love you SO MUCH xoxoxoxoxoxox

Honestly, I love you guys too. I'm glad I got that off my chest. And I'm sorry about the "you're not normal" comment, I only said that because I was upset. I want to be able to tell you guys things, but sometimes I worry that I'm this sex-obsessed freak and maybe I'm the one who's not normal. But if you don't look at me that way, then I won't either. ☺

Okay, I was reading back over this exchange and I have an idea. Can we not use the word normal? It's really subjective and it doesn't make anyone feel good.

Agreed! NORMAL SUCKS. Also let's never use the word slut. It's totally sexist and we — founders of The PAD and members of The Sisterhood of the Goat Mask — are anti-sexist!

I love this! Let's start a list of words we will not use in the PAD or life, if we can help it:

LOVE THIS!

- Normal
- Slut
- Prude

Oct 9

Good morning, Padlings! No big deal, but I walked home by myself yesterday because someone was waiting for someone else after basketball practice . . . Hoops? Any updates for us?

Can we please not make a big deal out of this? It's bad enough that JJ and all those guys were smirking at us and laughing from across the street. It's not like we were holding hands or anything, we just walked home together, side by side, like normal people. It was nice. The worst part was, my mom came barging out the front door before he could leave and insisted he come in for a snack.

OF COURSE SHE DID. I LOVE YOUR MOM SO MUCH. I would have done exactly the same thing. I can't wait to torture my own kids someday. What did he do? What did he say? Tell us EVERYTHING!

Sorry to disappoint you all, but there isn't that much to tell. We talked mostly about school and basketball. It was pretty normal, only I was super aware of his arm the whole time. It was really close. All the hairs on my arm were electrified or something. It was the weirdest feeling. I was worried he could tell and would think I was a weirdo. But then I couldn't exactly move my arm, because what if he asked me why I moved my arm?

SO CUTE! Do you think you have LOVE-MAGIC?

I wouldn't call it love-magic, but I admit he is pretty cute. And he was so good with my way-too-excited mother. She asked him about a hundred questions, like it was an interrogation. Seriously, she knew more about him in a half-hour than I do after knowing him all along! He even told her her beet hummus was the best he's ever had(!).

I've seen that boy eat, it's all Doritos and cheese strings. There is no way he's a hummus expert. I thought she was going to ask him to stay for dinner but he literally excused himself— that's what he actually said, "I have to excuse myself"— and left after maybe 15 minutes. I liked him before, but it made me like him even more. HELP!

Awwww! I think maybe I have a crush on Swoosh now?! Just kidding, he's all yours. You can have beautiful, tall, pro-basketball playing children and I'll play the piano at your wedding and people will ask about the tragic but beautiful spinster who plays such sad songs.

What is this, 1860? Dramatic much?

Wow, Swoosh is SO smooth, who knew?! I am seriously so happy for you. This is the best. Plus now you may have an actual date for the dance. Our first one of the year! Two weeks and counting!

Reminder, it's not just a dance, it's also a fundraiser. Does anyone want to help out? I'm in charge of decorations, but we need people to sell tickets and work at the refreshment table and monitor the halls. I had no idea there were so many moving parts for one little dance! It's so exciting to be behind the scenes and make it all work.

You tell us where to go and what to do and we'll be there, MP! I hope you don't have to spend the whole time working! Will they let you free for at least one dance? Sunny, what's going on with Violin Boy? Could you ask him?

OMG are you joking?! Nothing is going on! I don't even think he knows my name. Here is the full list of things we've said to each other

"Hi." (both)

"It's raining, did you bring an umbrella?" (me)

"Are you playing in the Harvest Recital?" (me)

"Yes." (Him. To the festival question. He just looked kinda startled when I asked about the umbrella.)

Maybe he's shy! Plus isn't your teacher always there? Maybe he feels weird talking to you in front of her. Or he's worried that he had a bad lesson and you heard the whole thing. Next time you should compliment his playing.

You should do more than that. You should exchange contact info. It's so much easier to message someone. If he's into you but shy, this could be the perfect strategy! Do it! YOUR FIRST KISS could be just a message or two away!

And how would I do that, just give it to him? In front of my music teacher

and my DAD?! I could never! I'd be too
embarrassed! Plus my mom is too nosy.
She's always hovering around when I'm on
my phone or my computer, like I'm going to
join a cult or get lured into a drug ring.
If she found out I was talking to a boy,
she'd be all over me. I'm doomed to never
be in love. At least until I'm out of the
house, and by that point I'll be too old
for anyone to ever look at me. Now I'm
depressed. 🙁

Don't be depressed, you're our Sunny! The
light of our lives! If Violin Boy can't see what
a ray of light you are, then it's his loss.

Speaking of love connections, what are you
doing tomorrow, Hoops? Are you at your
Dad's this weekend? My brother is having
some of his old basketball teammates over
to watch the Raptors game. He's deigning to
hang out with lowly middle schoolers again
since moving up to high school. Personally, I
think he misses being the big shot and this is
his way to feel like the big man again. Not that
he would EVER admit that.

Anyway, he mentioned that Swoosh is coming, so Hoops you should totally come too if you're here! You could hang out with him outside of school! At the very least, we can hang out and spy on them from my room.

MP! Look at you playing matchmaker! Hoops, you have to go! Test things out with Swoosh in a group scenario.

Test what things? We're barely "a thing." I only just realized that I like him and now you want me to crash a basketball party full of older guys and his friends? And do what, just hang around and watch them play 3 on 3 like a cheerleader?

YOU HAVE TO GO! It's not crashing if you live next door! And you just happen to be visiting your very best-est friend MP. In fact, it would be weird if you DIDN'T go. He knows where you live now, right? I bet he's secretly hoping you show up.

Plus you're an amazing basketball player. It would not at ALL be weird if you came to hang out. Actually, maybe I'll come, too. Sounds like there will be lots of boys and opportunities for Love-Magic to finally strike! Will a certain "very professional" Student Leadership member be there, MP?

The more the merrier, you should all come! And it's definitely not weird, Hoops. You wouldn't just sit and watch, obviously they'd ask you to play. But if it feels even the slightest bit weird, you and I can go do something else.

And since you must know, Veep is invited. He was on the basketball team last year with my brother. Not that it makes a difference to me, because I don't think about him like that, remember?

This is all very, very promising! I'm going to a party with my fun sister on Saturday, but otherwise I'd

totally come! Have fun! Break hearts!
Don't do anything I wouldn't do . . . or
wait . . . maybe you should! 😉

Wait, like an actual HIGH SCHOOL party?
What if there is alcohol there? OMG that
is so crazy! You're going to meet all these
cool older people and stop hanging out
with us. I guess it was only a matter of
time. 😖

Chill, Sunny! It's not like some big
rager with people making out in the
pool or throwing up in the sink or
anything. It's at her new boyfriend's
house, and it will just be a few
friends hanging out. Maybe there will
be alcohol there, but that doesn't
mean I have to drink. I'm a big girl.
I can take care of myself. Fun Sister
is cool. She would never pressure
me to do anything. I'm hoping she
has some equally cool, eligible guy
friends. Sounds like we all have very

promising weekends in the love-magic department, ladies.

Wow. I can't imagine going to a high school party. Aren't you even a little nervous? Also, I thought your Fun Sister liked girls?

She does, but she's with a guy now. She's bi, and totally open about it. She's open about everything, really. She is definitely the best part about our new living situation. She's like my hero! Plus her new boyfriend is really cool. He's kind of quiet, but he plays bass in a band and they're going to play at the party! Maybe he will have single bandmates? I can totally see myself dating a musician!

YOU ALL HAVE SUCH AMAZING PLANS EXCEPT ME! While you're at group dates and high school parties, I will be in a car on the way to see my grandmother next to my barfy brother who 100% will be carsick

BOTH WAYS! Please live your lives to the fullest so you can report back to me on Monday.

LET THE WEEKEND OF LOVE-MAGIC BEGIN!

Oct 12

Weekend recap, please! Don't spare any details! MP, have you changed your mind about dating now that you've spent some time with Veep outside of school? Hoops, did Swoosh offer to walk you home and then KISS YOU GOODNIGHT?!

Considering I live next door, it wouldn't have been much of a gesture. There was nothing date-like about any of it, actually. Swoosh pretends like he doesn't know me whenever the guys are around. So it was just a bunch of friends, hanging out. It was fun, but I was a little hurt at how he ignored my very existence. I guess I do like him. Help!

I KNEW IT!

As Hoops said, it was just a group thing, not date-like at all. There were fifteen people there including my little cousins, and they insisted we all play together at one point. It was so sweet to see all these hot-shot basketball players kidding around with them. Poor Hoops! I bet it wasn't the way you imagined spending time with Swoosh!

It wasn't a bad weekend, it just wasn't really date-like, which I guess I should have known. Everyone was nice and your cousins were really cute, actually. Also SOMEONE was definitely staring at our MP the whole time, not that she noticed.

OOOOOOH REEEEEEALLY?! Maybe you're not into him, MP, but just something to think about, if you decide maybe you would like to give kissing a try before high school. You could do a lot worse than our highly esteemed Veep! OMG, if you guys were official, Cheryl Blossom would actually die. And isn't that the best revenge for her completely uncool (and unsuccessful) attempt to throw you off your path to Student Leadership?

P.S. I'm sorry, Hoops, but Swoosh will come around. The dance is coming up, and that's the perfect opportunity for your first kiss!

I am choosing to be the bigger person and rise above the petty behaviour of bullies like Cheryl Blossom. Winning by my own merit was revenge enough for me!

XOXO
MP!

P.S. You are all kissing obsessed. I am advocating for a kissing-free zone in the PAD. For one whole week we will not discuss kissing.

LUV U!

I am into this! After Saturday I feel like maybe there won't be any kissing between me and Swoosh for a long time, or maybe ever. It's not like I wanted to hold hands or anything like that. I don't know. It was fun and everything, but maybe he's not as into me as I thought. Except now I am definitely into him! This sucks!

It's not you, it's Swoosh. He probably just wanted to look cool in front of the older guys. He's definitely 100% into you, Hoops. Maybe you should be the one to make the next move? Although I guess since there is a kissing ban, we won't be talking about it this week. BTW the ban is fine by me. It's not like I'm kissing anybody anyway.

If there's a ban on kissing then I can't tell you about my Saturday night . . . 😜

BAN REMOVED!

I want to hear about your high school party! Tell us more about FIFTEEN!

Who? → 15 as in years old?!

Okay, so Sunny knows some of this already because I knew she would appreciate a juicy update, being stuck with her barfy brother and senior citizens over the weekend. So I texted her the basics to give her a reason to live (jk)!

So Fifteen is this guy I met at the party on Saturday, which was SO AMAZING. Srsly guys, everyone was so nice, it was not intimidating at ALL, just cool people hanging out in the backyard with a real live band. You all would have been totally fine. Fifteen goes to school with my Fun Sister. He's got this messy, kind of rumpled look, but he smells amazing, like soap and cinnamon or something. Seriously standing next to him I thought I was going to faint, he smelled so good. Not at all like the guys in this class. Plus he has a lip ring, which I think is totally hot.

SO HOT!

Anyway, I was watching the band, and I saw him look at me, then look away. So we did that long-distance flirting thing for a few songs, and then when the band took a break I went to find my Fun Sister and suddenly he was right there! He asked if I liked the band, I said yes, and then we started talking about music and school and everything . . . until the kissing started anyway. 😏

I was joking about the teen movie thing before, but now it seems like you actually were in the middle of one! Wow! I guess now you have a new crush to replace Dimples with, which I am all for. I didn't want to say anything before because I know you like him, but you're way too good for him.

TEAM FIFTEEN!

Who cares about Dimples, I am Team Fifteen! I can't believe you just made out in the open like that. I would be way too embarrassed. Was there drinking?

Not really. Some people had coolers but nobody was drunk or anything. Fifteen and I were too busy talking. And then kissing, which is way better than talking (or drinking). 😊 Anyway, we've been texting ever since, which is why it is EXTRA CRUEL that we are not allowed to have our phones. Doesn't Mr M want me to achieve my goals?

Wow, well promise me you'll be careful! He's older, so he might have different expectations. Do you want me to ask my brother about him? Maybe he knows him or can scope him out for you.

Okay, MOM! Srsly MP, I have a mother and two older stepsisters. I don't need yet another person looking out for me. I'm a big girl, you don't have to worry about me! And trust me, there isn't anything your brother can tell me that my good friend the internet can't. I got this!

Oct 13

Today's question was a good one: DOES A BLOW JOB COUNT AS SEX? Short answer: yes! That's why it's officially called ORAL SEX. There are many forms of sexual activity that don't involve penis in vagina action (not Coach's exact words). Coach said the traditional definition of sex is limiting and HETERONORMATIVE (hello new favourite word!) because P in V sex doesn't include gay or lesbian people. Longer answer:

You shouldn't engage in any sexual activity until you're ready for it and being safe. Thoughts?

That makes sense. I would definitely classify anything with genitals as sex.

P.S. Heteronormative IS a good word! We already have a list of words never to be spoken by the Sisterhood of the Goat Mask, should we make a list of words we want to use more often?

um, obviously.

I love this idea! Can we add period? As in menstrual period, not the thing at the end of the sentence, obviously.

Also vulva and vagina, I get those two mixed up!

Same!

Def!

INTO IT! Can we also add menstruator? Like Hoops said, it's not just women who get their periods. Trans men and nonbinary people do too. I never realized how heteronormative (look I'm doing it!) things were until I met Fun Sister. Her partner started using they/their pronouns and some people have been so rude about it! Sometimes I slip up, but I'm getting better at it. They are probably the coolest person I know. They are just so totally themselves. I like them so much, maybe even more than Fun Sister sometimes. She wasn't as happy for me as I expected when I told her about Fifteen. Every once in a while she gets all condescending and tells me to "enjoy my youth" and "don't grow up too fast." She is only two years older than me. It's totally annoying.

Hoops and Swoosh, Twix and Fifteen, WHY DOESN'T THE WORLD WANT ME TO FIND LOVE?!

Sunny, quit complaining about your love life and do something about it! Talk to Violin Boy! Wasn't your goal to be kissed? You have to actually take the steps to achieve your goal. MP had to give a speech, which she hated, but now she's on SL and loves it. I didn't get the position I wanted on the team, but we are seriously good this year and we might just make it to county, and Twix is obviously going to be racking up the kisses now that she's got all this VIP access to high school parties. You can't just let things happen to you, you have to do something about it!

P.S. I like the word menstruator, it sounds like a cool job or a superhero name.

No matter the challenge, or the menstrual flow, THE MENSTRUATOR can handle it!

The Menstruator is here to help you with your problems, and your cramps!

YAAAAAS!

Love it!

Whoa, who is this new Hoops? I like her! And I totally agree. You have to talk to him, Sunny, ASAP! Don't you have piano tonight? Ask yourself, WHAT WOULD THE MENSTRUATOR DO?

Yes, but what would I say? I don't have anything planned! I can't just talk to him tonight for no reason!

P.S. Maybe The Menstruator gets their superpowers and their confidence from their period, which, REMINDER, I DO NOT HAVE YET!

Excuses, excuses!

Why not? Plus you have a reason, the reason is you like him! Of course you don't have to tell him that, but you need to at least give him some signs. Don't overthink it. Just be friendly and ask him a few questions. It doesn't have to be a big dramatic moment. You don't have to inhabit the fierce warrior spirit of The Menstruator. Approach the situation like

their everyday alter-ego, like Diana Prince
or Peter Parker.

Agree!

GO FOR IT, SUNNY D!

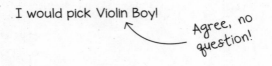

WYR have a simple conversation
with a boy you kind of already
know, or ask three people to dance
at the dance on Friday?

I would pick Violin Boy!

Agree, no
question!

Same! Those are my terms! Sunny,
you have to talk to Violin Boy tonight
and report back with an actual
conversation. If you don't, you have
to ask THREE people to dance at the
dance on Friday. Surely saying hi to
Violin Boy is easier than that!

OMG THAT'S SO MEAN! And not a fair WYR. It's not like any of you have to actually live with the consequences! I promise I will try to say something at music tonight, but if I freeze or start to laugh or do something embarrassing, IT'S ALL YOUR FAULT!

Oct 15

OMG I did it! I talked to him and we sort of have a date on Saturday? Well, not a date exactly, but the important thing is, I did it and I didn't die and he didn't laugh at me or look at me like I was a weirdo or anything like that!

I thought about what MP said, about asking questions and keeping it casual and non-dramatic, so when he came out from his lesson I just smiled like I knew him and we were already friends.

So, he looked a little surprised, but then he smiled back, and by some miracle, my music teacher asked if I could wait for five minutes because she had to make a call, and then she closed the door and we were alone together in the waiting room! It felt like it was meant to be, which made me feel way braver. Here is our exact conversation, word for word:

Brilliant!

           Me: Hey, what's up?

VB: Nothing. Just finished my lesson.

           Me: You sounded really good!

VB: Thanks. I don't really like the Bach that much.

           Me: Same. I mean, I don't like this sonatina I'm supposed to play at the recital in a few weeks. I don't have anything by Bach.

VB: That makes sense. Bach didn't really compose much for piano.

           Me: Right. So, doing anything fun this weekend?

VB: I'm taking music theory.
It starts on Saturday.
Will you be there?

AND I SAID YES! And do you know what he said? "GOOD!" not Okay, or Nice, or See you there, but GOOD! That's the best possible answer, don't you think?

Hurray, Sunny! I agree, "good" is the best possible answer. "Good" means he is glad you're going to be there and he wants you to know it! See? All you had to do is put yourself out there a little bit and look what happened!

GET IT, GIRL . . . THIS IS AWESOME! I knew he liked you. How could he not? Now all you have to do is wear something cute and make sure you sit next to him at theory or whatever it's called. This is like a serious YA romance style scenario here. I should know, since I am "reading more." I'd give you tips for your hot date, but you'd only overthink it (you know you would). Just be your cute self!

So it's definitely not a "date," because my piano teacher and a few other kids will be there, and also theory is basically music math and the last thing I need is another kind of math to fail. But also I'm really super proud of myself! I did it! AND I was having a good skin day! I feel amazing!

That could not have gone any better, Sunny, I'm so happy for you! And if you think about it, you're working on both of your goals — don't fail math AND get kissed! Maybe he can help you with your math? That's kind of romantic!

This is so crazy, the dance is tomorrow and then the next day is my first music math class with Violin Boy and yet I'm supposed to just sit here and think about my social studies project? SO MUCH IS HAPPENING!

What are you guys wearing to the dance? I don't have anything that's dance-worthy. I want to look a bit older, more like the kind of girl you would think about asking on a date after your music math class, or ask to dance, not someone forgettable or worse, who barely registers as a girl.

The B.B.W. STINKS!

Did I ever tell you about that time with the B.B.W. outside the washroom? I was about to go in and he said, "That's the girl's washroom," and I said, "Yeah, I know, I'm a girl," and then he looked at my chest in a really obvious way and said, "Are you sure?"

It was SO awful, I totally went into the stall and cried, only Cheryl Blossom and her minions came in, so I had to suck it up and pretend I had allergies. The worst part is he basically confirmed my greatest fears. Guys don't even look at me like a girl. I am so flat I could show up at the pool in swimming trunks and nothing else and everyone would think I was a boy (not that I ever would, obviously!).

Don't let the Big Bad Wolf bring you down, Sunny. He ruins everything around him, which is why we call him the B.B.W. Well, that and his very shaggy hair. What he said was cruel and untrue. Not only are you a girl, you are one of my favourite girls. xo

Mine too!

Me, three! You're SUPER cute, Sunny, and I know we can pull an outfit together that will ensure that everyone knows it on Friday. Seriously, now that there are three of us of a certain age living in my house, the wardrobe situation is out of control! Your killer outfit is hiding

somewhere in our closets, I know it!
Come over before the dance and we
can get ready together. All of you
should come!

You guys are the best! And, Twix, I would
love, love, love to come over and have you
dress me. You have the BEST style. Thank
you so much! Seriously, though, I think
everything would be a little bit better
if I had actual, noticeable boobs. Or any
boobs at all, really. That's what I would
wish for more than anything, you know, if
wishes actually worked.

I have the opposite problem. I would wish for
a smaller chest. Ever since I went up two cup
sizes I don't feel like me anymore, like my
body went ahead and changed into something
else without my permission. People look at
me differently too. They look me up and down
or sometimes their eyes will drift toward
my chest for a split second and I want to
scream, those are not important! I wish I

could hide them, but they're so obvious. Plus they're in the way 80% of the time. Even when I wear two sports bras they still bounce in a way that is more noticeable than I would like. I never told you this at the time, but last year Cheryl Blossom came up to me after gym and said, "Don't take this the wrong way, but we saw you running in gym and we think it's time you started wearing a bra." I was so ashamed! I'm still embarrassed writing it down here. Why does she hate me so much? I can't think of a single reason.

P.S. Tell no one!

SHE SAID WHAT? I can't believe that. Why didn't you tell me? That is SO mean and SO uncalled for! Your boobs are amazing and FTR I would switch chests with you ANY DAY.

I can TOTALLY hear her saying that! I'm so sorry, MP! But I swear it's not just you. She's been trying to freeze me out at basketball ever since Swoosh and I became whatever it is that we are. Last week, she went on and on about this bad smell in the change room and made this big show about trying to find the source, walking around and taking dramatic sniffs. Then she stopped right where I was changing and said, "You know, I can recommend a good deodorant," and then laughed like it was the funniest thing in the world. Why is she so mean? She is by far the meanest girl in our class.

P.S. FTR I DO wear deodorant.

That's because she's super jealous about your BOYFRIEND. We can call Swoosh that now, can't we?

No comment.

You guys are CRAZY. And you're both perfect, no matter what Cheryl Blossom says or does! I don't have luscious melons like MP, but I like my little strawberries just the way they are! But sometimes I wish I had better legs. Mine are both stumpy AND lumpy. I can never wear cute short-shorts like you, Sunny. I mean, I make do with what I've got — I know I'm gorgeous — but sometimes I think about what it would be like to have really long legs and a noticeable thigh gap.

I don't know what this says about me, but I've never thought about your legs before. They just seem like Twix's legs! I don't really think about my body that much, other than pushing myself to be a better player and improving my running times, but since we're being honest, I hate the way I smile in pictures. It's like my face doesn't know how to be natural. I see pictures of myself and I just want to cringe. I hope I don't look like that in real life.

P.S. Twix, please tell me you do not call your breasts your "little strawberries."

That is worse than the Little Red Engine and Aunt Flo combined times a million.

Let's agree to not refer to any of our breasts as kinds of fruit. At least not mine (I really hate melon).

Twix, I had no idea you ever felt that way. You're always so confident, as you totally should be. And Hoops, when I see you in pictures all I see is my beautiful friend. Isn't it crazy how the things we hate the most about ourselves don't even register with each other?

I think you look totally fine in pics, Hoops, but if you're worried about it I can give you some tips. It's all about angles and filters, baby. This convo is bringing me down. No more bad body talk! We have one more sleep til the most exciting night of the year so far (DANCE! DANCE! DANCE!) and we are all going to look KILLER.

P.S. Why shouldn't I call them strawberries? They're MY boobs!

STRAWBERRY BOOBS
A Poem by Twix

My strawberry boobs
are alright to me,
as perfect as a pair
of boobs could be.

You have truly outdone yourself.

You may have melons
or apples or cherries,
but I'm totally cool
with my awesome strawberries.

All boobs are different
and all boobs are fine,
but I love my boobs
because they are mine

I hate this but I also kind of love it?

LOL! I'm imagining strawberries wearing a bra!

Oct 16
*DANCE NIGHT!

Happy Dance Day! Only seven hours to go. Those seven hours are going to feel like a whole week, though. You're all coming for a slumbo, right? You can come over right after school and we can order food and get ready together. My Fun Sister is cool with us going through her closet. She has tons of stuff. She's practically a hoarder when it comes to clothes, plus you're basically the same size, Sunny, so her stuff should fit. Even better, Second Mom will not be there, so no hovering around all night telling us to keep it down. I SWEAR SHE WAS NEVER YOUNG. ←

Also, MP, I have lots of stuff that would fit you too. I'm not saying you need a makeover, but I have this V-neck that would be so totally cute on you if you would just let me style you this ONCE! It is a dance, after all, the perfect time to debut a new lewk. PLEASE!?!

I love this plan, only last night I kind of told Swoosh I would go to the dance with him . . . Don't get mad! It's making me nervous, TBH. I'd rather just hang out with all of you. Do you think it's rude if I tell him I'll meet him there? Or he can come meet me at your place, Twix? Actually, no, that would make him and me way too nervous to know you were all watching us from inside.

HOOPS, WHEN WERE YOU PLANNING ON TELLING US THIS VERY IMPORTANT INFORMATION?!? I told you that thing at MP's was just a blip, he totally likes you! Of course, you have to go with him! Don't worry about us. You can come over after the dance and give us a full update! I wonder who else is going to the dance with a date? Not a lot of other people in

our class I bet. THIS IS SO EXCITING!
Twix, I would LOVE, LOVE, LOVE to raid
your sister's closet. It's seriously a dream
of mine. Are you sure she won't mind? We
can take lots of cute pics to post so if
Violin Boy just happens to look me up, he
will be reminded of how cute I am.

Yay, Hoops! You're such a cute couple.
I agree with Sunny, you should go with
him. I can't come for dinner this time (or
personal styling, sorry, Twix) because I'm
on the decorating committee and we're
working right up until the dance starts.
But I will ask about staying overnight. We'll
all meet up at the dance and then after
we'll have all night for girl time.

Okay! Sounds like a plan. I don't think I've
ever been so excited for a dance before.
I've definitely never been this nervous. I
want to go with Swoosh, but I kind of
don't want to go with him?

If you don't go, you'll regret it. It's fine! It's a dance. It's not like anything is really going to happen with all those chaperones and people around. Last year they barely even dimmed the lights in the gym.

I can confirm that not only will the lights be off, but we're using the stage lights from the drama room for atmosphere. Veep insisted.

↑ "Veep INSISTED," did he?

DON'T START!

Thanks! I'm feeling extra nervous because I really don't know what to expect or how to act. This is my first sort-of-date, not counting the basketball game at MP's, which was definitely not a date. My stomach is all wonky. I can't tell if it's excitement or nerves or maybe both? I like him but I don't know if I'm ready for boyfriend/girlfriend stuff.

You can do it, Hoops! It's like the easiest, most low-key date ever. You'll only be alone for a little bit and then you're at the dance with all of us Padettes and most of the school. If you think about it, it's really similar to the group date (or whatever you're calling the thing at MP's), except you know for sure you'll get some one-on-one time with Swoosh and he won't act weird because it's not just his friends there watching. Hopefully they will be asking SOME OF US TO DANCE. Maybe Swoosh wants to take things slow, too. One more reason why you are perfect for each other! You can be slow and "go steady" together! (Get it?!)

Slow AND Steady WINS THE LOVE RACE!

Did you just call me a DATING TURTLE?

In a CUTE way!

You can always come find one of us if you're feeling like you need girl time or a break. I will be at the door for the first half of the night and then you can find me at the refreshment table. We're always happy to have an extra helping hand. But personally I think you're going to have a great night!

Wait, does that mean you're working the whole dance, MP? I know you are Miss Responsible, but you should at least get to enjoy the dance! The dance is for everyone! We are ALL going to have the best time! What is wrong with that clock, I swear it's going back in time. Hurry up, 3:30! We have some pizza to eat and make-up to do and HEARTS TO BREAK!

Oct 19

POST-DANCE RECAP! Okay, that Friday night was epic. I don't even know where to begin! Oh wait, yes

I do . . . remember when M "I don't think about boys" P got up close and personal with VEEP for the last slow song?! I had to take a pic in case when I woke up the next day I thought I was imagining things. It's pretty blurry, but I know what I'm looking at!

YAY! That was definitely one of the most fun parts of the dance for me! I'm not going to lie, when Veep came over to talk to me, a little part of me thought maybe he was going to ask ME to dance, but when he asked if I would watch the refreshment table for MP so she could dance, I was like, TOTALLY! I think this makes me your fairy godmother? Or maybe Cupid?

P.S. Twix, plz tell your sister I will wash her top and get it back to you later this week. Also tell her that I think she is a fashion icon and if she wanted to adopt me I would be totally cool with that.

Please, as if she's even noticed it's gone. What happened exactly, MP? We were all set to chat with you after the dance but you didn't respond to our texts. You didn't find someone cooler to hang out with, did you? Someone male, older and also an eligible member of Student Leadership? Someone VERY PRETTY? I wouldn't blame you if you did.

You didn't miss too much, just some bad singing and Sunny brought these face masks that practically burned our skin off. Although you DID miss a dramatic presentation of the epic love story of Hoops and Swoosh. 😜

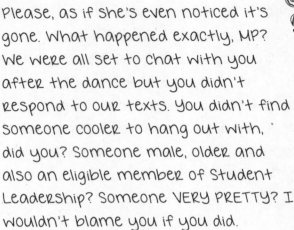

I still can't believe I let you guys read those texts from Swoosh. I don't know what came over me. Those are private! I feel so badly about it now. If you ever tell him about it I will say you stole my phone while I was asleep. No, I'll say you tied me up and stole my phone and I was forced to watch your sick little play. Actually, maybe I'll just deny everything.

You loved it, Hoops, don't deny it! You were laughing so hard! Don't pretend that Twix's portrayal of Swoosh wasn't totally believable and yet also somehow moving?! That voice! The hair toss! We'll have to do a revival just for MP. Twix, you should try out for the play. I know school participation is not "your thing," but you are reeeeeally good at impressions!

I don't need to be cast in some lame school musical to know I'm a star. 😜 Can we talk about how Cheryl Blossom asked Swoosh to dance right in front of you as if you weren't even there? And how Swoosh said "No, I'm with someone."

Actually, he said "I'm **KIND OF** here with someone."

Close enough. That's basically boy for I AM DATING THIS GODDESS YOU SEE BEFORE YOU AND I DON'T HAVE EYES FOR ANYONE ELSE, ESPECIALLY NOT YOU, CHERYL BLOSSOM!

(Okay, so he probably wouldn't have called her Cheryl Blossom. We're the only ones who do that.)

Sorry to disappoint you all, but it was just one dance, nothing more. I wasn't planning on dancing with anyone but, Sunny, you were so excited, and Veep was standing right there, and it felt cruel to say no. It was fine. But nothing is going on. Still not into Veep. Sorry to bail on the rest of the night, but I really wasn't feeling well and I ended up going straight home. I'm so sad I missed such an epic sleepover. Next time!

Twix, what happened with Dimples at the dance? I saw you dancing with him (pretty intimately, I might add). Are you getting back together? What about Fifteen?

It's not like we're OFFICIAL or anything, so I'm free to dance with anybody I want! I wasn't planning on dancing with Dimples, but I was kind of bummed that Fifteen wasn't there, and then our song came on and we both kind of found each other. It was nice, until MR. M was all "TOO CLOSE! TOO CLOSE," which was totally embarrassing and also totally untrue. I think Dimples wants to get back together, but mostly I was thinking about Fifteen. 😣

It was kinda true.

PG-14 at LEAST!! 😋

Um, we know how obsessed you are with Fifteen. You were looking at your phone half the night. It was kind of annoying, TBH. 😵

We were ALL looking at our phones! What about the whole text exchange with Swoosh? That was on a phone!

Why is that okay, but I'm not allowed to text Fifteen?

Because it was a group thing. We were all involved! It wasn't a super-secret private conversation in the middle of a sleepover. It sort of felt like you wanted to be hanging out with older, cooler people and that you were just putting up with us. At one point I thought you might ditch us to go hang out with him.

I don't think that at all! I had the best time! Sunny, you worry too much. And sorry if I was distracted, but the thing with Fifteen is new. He's not great at responding, so when he's live I feel like I have to strike while the iron is hot, you know?

Are we seriously fighting over phone stuff? I can't believe I'm saying this, but maybe there's something to Mr. M's

no phone philosophy! NEW PAD
RULE — NO PHONES AT SLUMBOS.
Or maybe we have designated phone
time, and then we put them away.

I like this idea a lot.

DEAL!

Fine, but can it be once an hour?
I'm VERY important and popular. 😜
Sunny, how was your first music
math class? And love connections
with Violin Boy? Did you get his
socials?

Kind of a letdown, honestly. Especially
after that epic Friday night! I was late,
so when I got there the only seat was
on the opposite end of the table from
Violin Boy. We didn't even speak. I tried
to make eye contact a few times, but I

had to lean forward and sort of crane my
neck to see him, so it was totally obvious.
Next time I am going to be early and will
loiter around the snacks until he arrives.
and then we can sit together.

P.S. Even the snack situation was boring.
At least that I can fix! Coming next week:
Sunny's Snack Makeover!

Oct 22

Happy Tuesday, Padettes! Today's
question was, Does it hurt the
first time you have sex?

If I was going to put a question
in the box, this would probably be
it. I'm not sure if Coach's answer
made me feel better, but nice to
know I'm not the only one who
worries about it. ☺

Me too! When you really think about it — the actual "P in V action," as Twix would say — it seems logistically impossible. How does it fit? I haven't worked up the courage to try tampons yet and they are definitely smaller than a penis. What did she say?

Coach said it doesn't have to hurt, and usually when it does, it means you need more lubrication. The vagina makes its own lubrication and when you're "aroused" (her word, not mine!), it coats the walls and makes it easier for the penis to slide in.

Haven't you ever had, like, a sexy dream or read something kind of hot and you get a little wet down there? According to Coach, that's your (vajayjay) telling you she's ready. Or at least interested. Coach also said the vagina is supported by a system

NOT Coach's words

LOL OBVI!

of muscles and can expand and contract to fit a penis or a baby during birth. That makes it all kinds of badass!

I can't believe we're talking about this, but I know exactly what you mean about the underwear thing. It's so embarrassing! I do my own laundry now so that my parents don't see any evidence in my underwear.

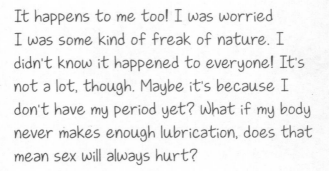

It happens to me too! I was worried I was some kind of freak of nature. I didn't know it happened to everyone! It's not a lot, though. Maybe it's because I don't have my period yet? What if my body never makes enough lubrication, does that mean sex will always hurt?

Coach said the first time can be uncomfortable, but it shouldn't be really painful, and that for most women it gets better once they know more about their own bodies. That's when she brought up The Big M.

I don't know what that means! I'm not in class, remember?

What Hoops is referring to is MASTURBATION. Coach said that touching yourself is a totally normal thing that can help you understand your own body and what feels good. What you like may be totally different than what Sunny likes. If you know what feels good, you can tell your partner and the whole experience is just better.

Add it to the list!   ✓Done.

Sorry, masturbation, I'm still getting used to the words! I saw lubricated condoms at Shoppers once, but I didn't really understand what that was until now. And before you ask what I was doing in that section, Swiftie dared me to go and read an entire package of condoms, front and back.

OMG, that's so funny! Swiftie is such a little troublemaker. Did you get caught? What did you do?

More importantly, what did you learn about condoms? 😊

Hahaha not much! There were twelve in the box and they were lubricated and "ribbed for HER pleasure!" Please don't ask me what that means. And they have an expiry date.

Coach also said there are emotional factors to consider. If you're not 100% ready or feeling uncomfortable, your vagina won't relax or it won't make enough lubrication and that's why it can hurt sometimes, which is why you should only have sex with someone you feel comfortable with and when you're truly ready.

AND THAT'S WHEN Sunny started
giggling and then asked for the
washroom pass and basically ran out
of the room.

I'M SORRY, I COULDN'T HELP IT! I
sort of pictured vaginas relaxing, like
at a spa, with fluffy white robes and
tropical drinks, and I couldn't stop
laughing! I'm so embarrassed. God,
what do people think? That I was
turned on IN CLASS or something? I
laugh at the WORST times!

I don't think **THAT** many people realized
you were laughing, so they probably
thought you just really had to go. Or
maybe that you were uncomfortable.

I can feel my cheeks getting red right
now, just reliving it. My body is such a
traitor! Let's talk about something else!

Okay good, because I need to ask your opinion on something. Do you think it's a bad sign that I haven't heard from Fifteen since Friday? Like, what was he doing over the weekend that he couldn't text me back? It's not like he was at school!

I'm sure it was nothing. Maybe he got busy or he's not really into texting. Maybe you stop trying for a bit and let him come to you. If he doesn't see how wonderful you are, he's not good enough for our Twix!

Boo, Fifteen! I thought older boys were more mature and would do things like text you back, but it's not like I have any actual knowledge or experience with that.

Whatever, I'm not going to worry about it too much. There are lots of guys in the world (like Dimples!). I'm going to make us an amazing and

empowering playlist with NO love
songs and NO male artists. We can
listen to it at lunch and remember
how awesome we are.

OMG Yes!! Can we give you suggestions?

Sometimes Swoosh gets distracted and
doesn't get back to me right away. Maybe
Fifteen has a part-time job? Or he had a
family thing? My mom doesn't let me take
out my phone at all when we're at my
grandparents' house.

P.S. How are you making this playlist?
You're not supposed to have your phone.

"Not supposed to" isn't exactly a
hard no. 😊

Don't worry about it. MR. M's not
even looking at me. I'm not one of
his favourites. As an academic lost

cause I basically don't exist to him. We're good. And don't worry, Sunny, I know what you like and I promise there will be at least two Taylor songs. The Maxi-PAD playlist will be the playlist to end all playlists. There's going to be something for everyone.

MAXI-PAD HAHAHA I LOVE IT! P.S. Lizzo too?

"This playlist is super-absorbing."

"Listening to Maxi-PAD gives you wings and makes you feel like you can fly."

LOLOLOL

Sadly, I have an SL meeting. I really wish I could be with you at lunch. I need some time with my girls and I could use an empowering playlist right now. There's a lot going on. Sometimes I feel like I can't keep up.

And this, coming from our very own super genius! You take all this school stuff too seriously, MP. You need more downtime! Skip it and let the Maxi-PAD playlist absorb your sorrows. We barely see you these days outside of the PAD, which isn't like in person, so it doesn't really count. Plus we didn't get quality slumbo time with you! We're overdue for some QT! 😊

OMG yes, can you please skip it? It's only one meeting! We miss you! We aren't the same without you! Plus — no offense — I don't think anybody would care if you weren't at one little meeting. Tell them you're not feeling well or you have to tutor your best-est friend Sunny so she doesn't fail her math test and lose all of her "social privileges" (obviously, my mom's words).

P.S. Srsly though, are we still meeting in the library after school tomorrow? I can't fail this test! 🙁

You know what? I will! Sometimes Danika misses a meeting because of choir. Why shouldn't I miss a meeting this one time? They don't know that I DON'T have another commitment . . . although I don't want to lie. Maybe I'll just not go and hope they don't ask.

And, Sunny, don't worry, I have you written down in my planner for tomorrow with little suns and hearts written around it. You're not going to fail this test!

Um, who are you and what have you done with my next-door neighbour? I'm totally kidding, just surprised! And I agree with Sunny, I doubt anyone would care that much. Lunch just got so much better!

Oct 21 ✉️

OMG here we go about Internet safety again. Do they think we were born in, like, the 90s? I don't even think Coach knows half of the things she's talking about. Would you ever send a pic to a guy?

You mean like a sexy pic? No. I would feel too weird. I can't imagine posing for it, even. I'd probably laugh or make my weird photo face. Ugh! Why is it so bad?! Plus what if the guy I sent it to showed it to a bunch of other people?

I love your face! Your face is beautiful! I might send one, if I really trusted him and we were officially together. Not that there would be much to look at.

Sunny, you shouldn't worry about your boobs. It's all about angles, anyway. Or you could take a picture of another part of your body. It doesn't have to be all about cleavage.

I definitely would do it. I think it's empowering, like here is this amazing picture of me, you should feel lucky that I'm sharing it with you. I've sent fifteen photos. Nothing TOO sexy, mostly just me looking cute in this blue top I love. You know the one. I wore it to the dance.

P.S. I finally heard back from him. He said his weekend was 'stacked,' whatever that means. We're all good!

Swoosh and I send photos too. Nothing sexy, just like, pics of where we are or what we're doing.

Sorry this took me so long to pass back, but I literally screamed a little when I read your entry! Bowtie thinks I'm totally crazy now and I think Coach heard so I had to put the PAD away and try to look like I was thinking about something other than HOOPS SENDING SWOOSH SEXY

PHOTOS. But what do you expect when I just found out two of my best friends are sexting!!

That is NOT what it is! It's regular pics, not sexy at all. I can show you the photos at lunch. It's, like, Swoosh making weird faces walking home and stuff. It's mostly boring, but also kind of cute? Mostly we try to make each other laugh.

I guess this means things are going well with Swoosh! I knew he liked you. But aren't you worried that it will escalate and he'll ask you for a more revealing picture? How will you say no?

Just like that — no! Plus it would be over text, so it wouldn't be that hard. I don't think Swoosh would ask. He's really sweet. Every day I like him more. And if he thinks I have "stupid photo face" he never says it.

That's because you don't, you goddess! My photo doesn't count as sexy. I would totally post it on Insta and I wouldn't get into trouble or anything. Plus I looked REALLY GOOD. Why can't I be proud of a really good photo? It's my body. I can share it with whoever I want!

But what if you break up and he turns out to be a jerk and he wants something from you and threatens to use the photo?

That's the actual definition of blackmail and I'd go to the police! Or a guidance counsellor or someone like that.

Even if it means you have to tell them about (or even worse, show them!!!) the photo? I don't know if I could do that.

So what, you let a jerk get away with being a jerk?

You make it sound so easy! I'm not as brave as you guys. Sometimes it's hard to say no, especially if you want someone to like you. I guess I'm just extra-sensitive to peer pressure or whatever.

Speaking of asking things, I know it's going to be lame, and it's mostly little kids, but will you guys come to my recital on the 31st? I know it's Halloween but the concert's at 2:30 and will be done in like an hour. Plus there will be snacks!

Of course we'll be there, with or without snacks. But snacks are nice. Are you making any of these snacks? (Please say junk bars!)

I would never miss an opportunity to see THE Violin Boy in person. He's going to be there too, right? Maybe I'll introduce myself. 😜

I will definitely be bringing snacks! And YES Violin Boy will be there, and NO, Twix, you absolutely cannot talk to him. I would die. You can't miss him, he's like the star pupil. Plus he's the really cute one, so it'll be very obvious.

Oct 22
(aka Sunny's Last Day of Freedom)

MP, where were you yesterday? I waited for you in the library for twenty minutes. I'm really worried about the test today. If I fail, I can't do anything fun like sleepovers or go out for Halloween or stay for any of Hoops' basketball games. It will be all math, all the time! I'll never get to see any of you!

I'm so, so sorry, Sunny! I completely forgot. I got caught up in a meeting. I know that isn't an excuse. I'm really, really, sorry. How can I make it up to you?

What kind of meeting? It's not like you to forget. I don't think you get how much harder school is for me. I'm not a super genius like you. You're always studying but the hilarious thing is you don't even really need to.

I don't think you know how bad my marks are. Not all of them, but a LOT of them. Like I can't even tell you how bad they are because I don't want you to think I'm too stupid to be friends with. ☹

FTR I do not base my friends on their marks. How can you think that?! Who cares about school! It's just a temporary holding pen for kids. Your real life begins after school, as an adult. There are SO MANY people who do rad things who were epically, famously bad at school. Didn't Einstein fail math? And he's an actual genius! Maybe you're a secret math genius, Sunny, and this place is just holding you back.

It is 100% holding ME back, which is why I'm going to meet Fifteen after lunch, so I won't be in French today.

P.S. Tell no one!

I think you know what my feelings are about truancy, Twix, so I won't go into it here. We will just have to agree to disagree, but I have to tell you as a concerned friend who thinks you only deserve the best that I am not sure I like this "Fifteen." Was this his idea? He didn't have the decency to text you back all weekend and then, when he does get back to you, he asks you to skip class? He doesn't seem like a great influence. Even Dimples wouldn't skip class!

P.S. Sunny, I'm so, so sorry. I can't tell you how sorry I am, you just have to believe me! I can help you at lunch, I promise!

I can help too! My marks aren't as good as MP's, but they're decent. We can have our own mini math club. It'll be fun, I promise!

No one thinks you're stupid, Sunny. You're good at lots of things — math is just one thing that you're not so good at. And the stuff we're doing is really hard right now. I'm practically failing French, if it makes you feel any better.

I can't believe you're actually skipping class, Twix. What will you say if someone sees you? Where are you and Fifteen going? Are you coming back for the math test? Actually, don't tell me. I don't want to lie if anyone asks where you are. I don't care if you skip. I just don't want to be involved.

Oh so **NOW** you like Dimples?! Chill, nobody's going to interrogate any of you or make you swear on a Bible or anything. I will just have to tell you about how I'm meeting him at the DQ for lunch (well, his lunch, our sixth period) AFTER the fact — OOPS! SORRY. ☺

It's not like we're doing anything important in French right now. I might miss the math test. It depends on how things go with Fifteen and how long he wants to hang out. It's just one test. Mr. M will give me some sort of make-up assignment that will probably be easier anyway. Why is it cool for MP to skip SL but not for me to skip possibly the most useless class (no offense to the French people or their language)?

Here I am worried about failing class and you might not even show up! Aren't you worried they'll call your mom? My mom would kill me if she found out I'd been skipping. Then she'd bring me back to life just to punish me some more. PROBABLY WITH MATH WORKSHEETS.

Thanks for wasting your lunch teaching me how to graph stupid integers, guys. I've even been dreaming about math class.

I had a dream that I showed up at school and the test was in another language, but not a recognizable one. It was just scribbles and gibberish. It was so real!

Don't worry too much about your dreams, Sunny. They're just dreams, they aren't real. It wasn't a sign that you are definitely going to fail. We'll help go over and over the math until you feel good about it and it will be fresh in your mind for the test.

Actually, you can learn a lot from your dreams. It's how your subconscious talks to you. I was reading this book on dream interpretation and apparently you can't dream in colour. And you can't die in a dream, because that means you die in real life. In this case, I think the meaning is pretty obvious. Sunny's stressed about the test. I wish I could pass on some of my excellent not-caring skills to you!

I see you've expanded your reading list from sexy YA to dream theory, so you must care about your goals and therefore school a little bit, Twix! I still can't believe you're skipping class. Maybe school isn't always fun, but that doesn't mean it isn't important. Is it going to become a habit?

P.S. Are you sure about the black-and-white part? I swear I dream in colour.

Me too! I swear the lines on the graph were bright red, which made them seem angry and therefore worse! Oh well. Have fun, Twix. I promise I won't tell anyone anything. Oh, and I have music math tonight (rescheduled because of the Harvest recital — you guys are still coming, right?), so today is basically National Math Day, aka the worst day ever.

But this means you get to see Violin Boy tonight! Also you don't know yet if you're going to fail the test. Never underestimate

the brilliant tutoring skills of me and
MP. Seriously, for someone who chooses
to call herself Sunny you're being pretty
depressing. We're going to have to start
calling you Gloomy.

P.S. Don't think I didn't notice you dressed
up a little today. You always dress up
when you have a music lesson. Looking
good, Sunny!

Oct 23

I was right. Yesterday was the worst
day ever. Not only did I probably fail that
test (sorry, guys, it wasn't your tutoring,
I'm just that dumb), but I almost killed
Violin Boy last night!!!

So, at the last music math class there
were these awful dry ginger things
(I refuse to call them cookies), and I
thought for the last class, I would bring
my own cookies, you know, to improve the
snack situation and also so Violin Boy could

see that I am good at some things, mostly baking. So I brought some of my chewy ginger-molasses cookies so VB could see what a real ginger cookie should taste like. At the break, VB took a bite of a cookie and he got this weird look on his face. I thought maybe they were dry or something, but then I remembered that I tested a few at home and they were some of my best cookies ever, not to brag or anything. Then he said, "Are these the cookies I brought?" and I said No, that I made them. And he went all shaky and asked if they were gluten-free BECAUSE HE'S CELIAC!!!

Apparently the dry ginger things were his special gluten-free cookies! He rushed to the bathroom, probably to spit out my POISON COOKIES, and then he called his mom and he had to leave immediately. After he left, our music teacher gave this little speech about safe snacks. She gave it to everyone, but it was obvious she was talking directly to me. I was the only one who brought an entire

Tupperware full of
POISON COOKIES!!

I was so mortified! I had no idea! What if he had to go to the hospital? He could still be there RIGHT NOW! Of all the people to poison! Why couldn't it be some random kid? Sorry, I know that's not nice, but srsly? Did it have to be VIOLIN BOY? My greatest gift is now the thing that may have KILLED the one boy I really liked!

Oh no, Sunny, that truly sucks. I'm so sorry. But if it makes you feel any better, I doubt he was rushed to the hospital. My mom has a gluten intolerance, which I know isn't the same thing as celiac, but you definitely didn't kill him! If she eats something with gluten in it, she mostly gets bloated or a really bad stomach ache. Sometimes she throws up or gets constipated, and this one time she had really bad diarrhea, but she's never been rushed to the hospital or close to death. He only

had a little bite before spitting it out,
right? He definitely won't die.

OH SO GREAT, NOW I'M THE GIRL
THAT GAVE HIM THE RUNS! How
romantic! He's never going to want to
speak to me again. Which is just fine,
since I can't bring myself to look at him
again. Oh well, at least I can drop Music
Math. Please, please can we talk about
something else?

Sunny, I'm so sorry! That is a really bad day.
There's no other way to look at it. Some
days are just bad. But you shouldn't blame
yourself for not knowing that he has celiac
disease. Really, your music teacher should
have mentioned something about the safe
snacks way earlier. I'm sure he's okay. Maybe
you could make him a get well soon card?
You're such a good artist!

Okay, out of respect for Sunny's truly bad
day, let's change the subject! MP, what's

going on with Veep? And before you say Nothing, we all saw you at the dance, and Wednesday I saw you leave the student council office together, just the two of you, and you were totally blushing! FESS UP!

Wait, THIS Wednesday? Is that why you missed our tutoring session? Because you had a meeting with Veep? I can't believe you ditched me for a boy, that's so not you.

I KNEW IT! YAH! Get it, girl! Veep is too pretty to ignore, even for someone as level-headed as you, MP! This reminds me of how Hoops kept telling us there was nothing going on with Swoosh and now they're all dancey-dancey and kissy-kissy and sexty-sexting.

THEY WEREN'T SEXTS

What do you mean you saw us? Were you spying on me? Am I not allowed to talk to boys now without it being a sign of something? We are in Student Leadership together, obviously we're going to have to talk to each other and, yes, even walk out of rooms together sometimes. I'm not boy crazy like all of you, not everything is an opportunity for kissing.

Whoa, calm down! Who said anything about being boy crazy? And I wasn't "spying" on you, I was in the hall. It's not illegal to be in the hall at lunch. Plus you were definitely red. It was cute! It's okay to have a crush, MP!

I don't know what you thought you saw, Hoops, but it wasn't anything romantic or scandalous, it was just regular school stuff. You know, some of us work really hard to do nice things for the school, like dances and yearbook, and everyone just rolls their eyes at us and treats us like suck-ups or nerds. It's hurtful.

Who said anything bad about student council or yearbook? I love the yearbook! I'm just saying I thought I saw something between you two and it was cute, but I'm sorry for being interested in my friend.

I hate it when we fight! No fighting, my recital is coming up and I'm super nervous and very sensitive to other people's moods. I read that acne can be caused by stress and this is stressing me out and I don't need ANY MORE SKIN PROBLEMS, thank you very much. There is nothing going on between Veep and MP, the end! So for the sake of my recital skin, can we just hug it out and talk about something else? xoxoxo

Is this recital an invite-only situation or can I bring someone? Maybe I could invite Fifteen and you could all see that he's not such a bad influence. I even made it back in time for the math test, which I

most definitely failed (you're not the only one, Sunny). But if Violin Boy is REALLY that cute, maybe I should ditch Fifteen and come on my own . . . just in case Violin Boy is kiss #5 (or 6, if you count Nahem the Chin Kisser).

P.S. I'm kidding, obviously. 😜

No comment.

YOU KNOW I HATE THAT!!!

Hi girls,

I think it's wonderful that you are writing and expressing yourselves and I hope you continue to do so, in this diary, or elsewhere. I just don't want to see the diary during class again, understood?

Coach Anderson

OMG OMG I'M SO SORRY! I got so caught up in our convo I didn't realize she had called my name. I almost died when she asked me to bring the PAD to her after class. I am SO SO SO SORRY, please forgive me!

It's okay, Sunny. It could have been a lot worse. I'm so glad it was Coach and not Mr. M. Do you think she read any of it? I hope she didn't read anything about Swoosh. It's not like we're trying that hard to keep people's identities secret and with all the basketball stuff she would definitely figure it out. How am I going to look at her at practice?

Of course she read it! How could she not? She's a teacher! This is exactly what I was afraid of. Sunny, how could you be so careless? I told you how important it was that we don't get caught. I don't think I can be a part of this anymore, it's too risky.

I know, I know, I'm such an idiot! I won't do it again. Please don't leave, MP! You have every right to be totally mad at me, but the PAD isn't the same without you. If it makes you feel any better, I don't think she had time to read much of it. She only kept it over the break. I think she just wanted to scare us a little. I'M SO SO SO SORRY. PLEASE FORGIVE ME!!!

MP, relax! Coach is totally fine with it. She basically told us to keep doing it, only be sneakier. We can be sneaky! I am the QUEEN of sneaky! It's fine! You're fine! Even if she did read it, or some of it, it's not like we said anything bad about her. We're very pro-Coach. Imagine if Mr M had found it? Or Cheryl Blossom? That would be something to actually freak out about.

That's what I mean! I don't want to be involved in gossip and rumours or any rule-breaking. I don't want Coach or anyone to think badly about me, or any of us. They'll take it out of context. Plus what if she tells my parents? Or lets them read the PAD? That is the worst thing that could possibly happen. They'd never understand! I really don't think I can be part of this anymore. Maybe you think I'm overreacting, but I know what could happen if my parents found out.

I think we all need to calm down. If anyone should be embarrassed it's me, since it's pretty obvious who Hoops and Swoosh are. But seriously, read what she said. She thinks what we're doing is WONDERFUL! That's her word, not mine. She would tell us if she wanted us to stop. I do think we should lay low for awhile, though, just in case. Will that make you feel better, MP?

I don't know. Maybe.

P.S. It's lie not lay. Remember, chickens lay, people lie.

Chickens lay,
people lie

Are those chickens supposed to be dead?

No they're laying!

Right, but doesn't laying mean laying eggs?

OMG IT DOES! I FORGOT!!
HAHAHAHAHAHAHA

Guys you are nerding out so hard
right now, I can't even. Cool drawing,
though, Sunny D!

Oct 23

Okay, it feels WEIRD in here right now.
What's going on? What did I miss? Did
something happen during sex ed?

I think we're all still reeling from the question box. Today's question was, "What do you do if you think you're being harassed, but you can't prove it?" Intense, right?

SO intense. Do you think someone is being harassed right now in the class? Or maybe it's one of those hypocritical questions, like the one about getting pregnant on your first time?

I think you mean hypothetical, not hypocritical, Sunny. That's a pretty serious question. What did Coach say?

She said you should talk to an adult that you trust, like a parent or a guidance counsellor. She also put a list of websites and phone numbers on the homework board for people to check out if they want to talk to a professional or are in crisis. They're still up there, under the date. She was calm and everything, but you could tell she was worried. She said whoever put the question in the box should feel comfortable going to her, if they wanted. Who do you think it was?

It's hard to tell. Swiftie looks kind of sick to her stomach, don't you think? Even Cheryl Blossom was quiet. Normally she smirks and looks at her minions during question box time, but she just looked straight ahead. It could be anyone.

I feel sick to my stomach too! I don't want to think of something like that happening to anyone in this classroom, or anyone anywhere, ever! How am I supposed to focus on anything else? How can we just go to French like nothing happened? What would you guys do, if it was you?

I would probably tell Second Mom first. My Fun Sister would turn it into, like, a protest or big public campaign or something, but Second Mom would get to the bottom of it right away, no fuss. I complain about her a lot and she's a nightmare most of the time, but she's also really badass and would know what to do in any situation. She is the person I'd want to be with during a zombie apocalypse for sure.

I guess I would tell my mom, but it's hard to imagine it. It's just the two of us and she already feels guilty about working all the time. It makes her hypersensitive and she'd probably blame herself for not being around more, or something. Then I'd feel even worse! I can totally see her crying and following me around for days. She'd never let me out of her sight again. And you KNOW she would make it her mission to ruin the life of whoever was harassing me. Fuss is kind of her middle name.

It's kind of nice that she'd make such a fuss and to know she loves you and cares about you that much. I'm not sure I would tell anyone at all. I guess it depends on how bad "IT" is. How do you know if something is actual harassment? If it was even a little murky, I don't know that it would be worth it to tell anyone. You all know how I crack under pressure, I would giggle or be dumb or tell it all wrong.

Even if I was telling the truth, people might not believe me. That would be the worst thing. That this awful thing happened and I worked up the courage to tell someone, but then no one believed me, or they think it's no big deal. I'd feel so stupid. Maybe it's better to deal with it on your own and go to therapy when you're older. Therapists are literally paid to believe you.

Sunny, I hope you know that I would believe you, and I bet all of

the members of the Sisterhood
of the Goat Mask would! At the
very least, you could call the
hotline Coach put on the board.
It's totally anonymous and you'd
be talking to a professional who
knows exactly what to do or say.
The thing that makes me the
saddest is that whoever put the
question in the box obviously
thinks they don't have anyone to
talk to.

Or maybe they're not sure if what happened
was actually bad enough to report. Maybe
the police or the authorities don't think
some things are as bad as others, like Sunny
said. There must be an official list or scale,
but how do you know what it is? Let's say
someone grabbed you, or tried to kiss you.
Obviously that's not as bad as rape, even if
it was unwanted and made you feel violated.
How do you know if something is actually
criminal or just not appropriate?

It's not about being appropriate or having nice manners! Even if it's not "rape," if you don't like that it's happening, it shouldn't happen. Aren't there laws about that? I would tell someone. Maybe not the police, but an adult. At the very least I'd call the hotline, like Twix said.

Mr. M keeps looking over here. Do you think Coach told him about the PAD? Maybe I should put it away for now. I'll write more later.

Oct 26

Okay. Okay, can we talk about today's sex ed class? It was the best one yet. All that stuff about consent! I can't believe that some people think it's okay to just assume things about other people's private parts. What did Coach say, "A kiss is not a permission slip for the rest of your body?" I love that!

I LOVE THAT TOO! I want a T-shirt with that on it. Or a really cool locker poster. Coach is such a badass. She reminds me of my fun sister sometimes but, like, older. She was really fired up today.

Obviously, she's fired up about THAT QUESTION. You know what really got me? "Silence doesn't mean yes." I never thought about it like that before. The whole point of a yes or no question is there are only two answers. It's like a WYR. You have to pick one. There's no in between, unless you're trying to bend the rules. And you can't bend the rules with consent.

I can't stop thinking about THAT QUESTION. Someone in this very room right now put it in the box. Someone in this room RIGHT NOW is going through something really, really bad. Doesn't it feel like we should be doing something more?

Like what, launch our own private investigation? People just don't talk about things like that. Okay, maybe this is a bad thing to even suggest, but what if it's not real and it's just some jerk trying to stir things up with a fake question? Someone like B.B.W. or Cheryl Blossom? You know they are both totally capable of it. Think of all the mean things they've done, and that's just to us! Cheryl lives for rumours and it's all anyone is talking about right now. It's like Rumour City around here.

I know, and I did hear something, but I don't believe it. Just so you know, Hoops, some people think that you put THAT question in the box. I would feel like a very bad friend if I didn't ask, so is everything okay with you and Swoosh? Was that your question?

What? Where did THAT come from? It was 100% not me who put that question in! Is that what people are saying? Swoosh

barely looks at me at school! We haven't even held hands! Even at the dance we were way more PG than Twix and Dimples (sorry, but it's true!). How can anyone think that? How can you think that?

I heard that too. But I didn't believe it. I figured it was just because you are the only couple in our class at the moment (that we know about), so people just assumed it was you. Plus Coach did say that the majority of sexual assaults happen between people who are close or have a personal relationship. I guess people took that to heart and then looked around the room and you're the first couple that came to mind. I'm really glad it's not you, Hoops, even though I knew it probably wasn't.

I'm so sorry, Hoops! I never really thought it was about you and Swoosh, but I wanted to check JUST IN CASE, plus I thought you should know what people are saying! And okay, this isn't very nice, but I bet Cheryl Blossom is behind it. She was trying so hard to get Swoosh away from you at the dance and has basically been glaring at you ever since. It's not like she hasn't spread rumours before. Remember when she told people I was addicted to my inhaler? She basically called me a drug addict!

Don't worry, Sunny, nobody took that rumour seriously. You can't get addicted to an inhaler. It's not the right kind of drug. Cheryl Blossom is definitely not one of my favourite people, but to start a rumour like that might be the worst thing she's ever done. It could ruin Swoosh's life.

We have to kill that rumour. It's totally unfair to Swoosh, and I don't want to be part of it either! Do you think I should tell him about it? He can be kind of clueless sometimes. Certain things go right over his head.

Definitely tell him! Plus then you can talk about boundaries in your own relationship, like Coach says. And maybe he knows something we don't. He could have some valuable Boy Intel.

I'd want to know, wouldn't you? Plus he's your boyfriend now — you have to tell him things like this. It proves you're worried about him, and that you're sticking by him. He has to know that YOU don't believe it.

Um, no, Twix, I am not using an awkward conversation about someone starting a rumour about him being involved in sexual harassment to talk about our own boundaries. But I'll tell him the bit about the rumour. He's going to be so upset!

Oct 27

So I talked to Swoosh. It was pretty awkward at first, but it got easier the more we talked and it ended up being a really good conversation. He was obviously super upset that anyone would think that about him, but when I told him that most didn't believe it, he calmed down a bit. I asked him if the boys had heard anything about THAT question, and he said they really don't talk about stuff like that, but he and JJ talked about it privately and they both thought it was a big deal and he swore they would never do anything like that.

He did tell me one surprising thing, though. Twix, he said he saw you put a question in the box just the day before THAT question was pulled. I didn't believe it at first, since you've been making fun of the question box and don't really take school stuff that seriously, but then I thought maybe you didn't want to tell us because the question was so serious. So I guess what I'm asking is, was it you, Twix? Do you need help? Is everything okay with Fifteen? He's a lot older than you. Has he been pressuring you? Did something else happen when you skipped class? You haven't really talked about it much.

Um, wow, okay. What makes Swoosh so sure I was putting a question in the box and not handing in an assignment? It's right next to Mr. M's inbox on his desk! Even if I did put something in the box, I swear to you that I did not ask that question. There is nothing like that going on with me, with Fifteen or any other guy. Just because he skips school sometimes doesn't mean he's a creepy predator. And he's barely two years older than us. You all talk about him like he's a dirty old man.

And the reason I didn't talk about it much is because it wasn't that big a deal. It was just the two of us at lunch, but then he wanted to show me the ramp he and his friends built behind the hardware store, the one near the DQ. (Before you call him a delinquent, his uncle is the manager and said they were fine to skate back there!)

It was okay at first, but when more of his friends showed up I got kinda bored. It wasn't funny or romantic and so I didn't think it was worth mentioning it. Plus you guys made such a big deal about me skipping in the first place. So can we let this go? I swear on the PAD that I did not put that question in and everything is fine. Are we good?

Okay, that sucks and everything (Boo, Fifteen!), but you never really answered the question. Did you put something in the question box? I thought the point of the PAD was to share our true feelings and talk things out. I tell you guys everything in here, even the really embarrassing stuff! Don't you trust us? Would you seriously rather have Coach read your question aloud and answer in front of the class than write it here in the PAD? Hoops is right, it's out of character for you to put a question in the box. Unless something is really wrong, and if it is, we want to help! We're the Sisterhood of the Goat Mask, you say it all the time! What kind of sisterhood doesn't tell each other the truth and support each other when things are bad? xoxo

No, the point of this stupid diary is to have something interesting to do in class since they took our phones away. But, honestly, I'm getting pretty tired of constantly being judged for my choices. For the last time, I did not put that question in the box, and if I did put something in, it's none of your business, OKAY?

That's not the only reason for the
PAD and you know it, Twix. We're not
being "judgemental," we are being your
friends who care about you! Why is it
okay for you to tease MP about Veep
or keep pushing me about Swoosh or get
mad whenever I write "no comment," but
when I ask you a serious question about
something that I really and truly care
about, you're allowed to get pissy? It's
a total double standard and it drives
me crazy.

!?!

Well, it certainly FEELS judgemental,
and TBH, maybe I don't want you to
know about my life. You're all such
goody two-shoes. It's like I have to
be careful about who I am around
you. Maybe I'm outgrowing this stupid
diary. Maybe I'm outgrowing you.

I hate when you pretend like the PAD is
this stupid, childish thing. It's not just a
diary, it's the PAD, and it means a lot to

me. I don't have anywhere else to talk
about these things. Deep down I was
always a little worried that you saw me as
immature, Twix, but it really hurts to see
it in writing. I can't help it that I'm not
as cool as you or that I don't have older
stepsisters to take me to high school
parties or that my parents will ground me
if I fail math. Those are just the facts
of my life, and if you can't accept that,
then why are we friends at all?

Please don't fight, I need the PAD too, and I
need all of you, especially right now. It was
me, okay? I put the question in the box. I
knew if Coach pulled it, you would write about
it here and then I might have a better idea of
what to do.

I wanted to tell you about what was going on,
but I didn't know what to say. It's probably
easier for me to just write it here. So here
goes . . . I put the question in the box because
Veep has been bothering me. Or something, I
don't even know if that's the right word. Most

people would probably think I'm overreacting, which is why I didn't say anything before.

At the dance, he kept asking me to dance and I kept finding other things to do so I could say no. But then when he got Sunny to look after the refreshment table and you came running over all giddy and excited, I couldn't exactly say no without looking like a horrible person.

During the dance, I kept leaning back, trying to put more space between us, but he would just step closer. Too close. I could even smell the dill pickle chips on his breath. I felt totally trapped. Then he kept moving his hands lower until they were no longer on my waist and then there was a definite . . . butt squeeze. When the song finally ended, he just turned and left without a word. I was confused. It happened so fast! It couldn't have been an accident, right? Do you think I'm overreacting? Be honest.

MP! I HAD NO IDEA, I'm SO sorry! I thought I was being helpful that night! I thought it was so sweet when Veep asked me to watch the refreshment table so you could dance. I thought I was playing a part in this big romantic gesture! I had NO idea you didn't want to dance with him or that I was basically setting you up for an unwanted butt squeeze! That is SO NOT COOL! You are definitely not overreacting, you are acting like a person who has been groped without consent!

Agree, you definitely can't "accidentally" squeeze someone's butt. How would that even work? What, you had an involuntary hand spasm and suddenly you have a handful of someone's butt? Dimples' hands were definitely on my butt at one point during our dance, but he knows I'm down with a little butt squeeze because we've talked about it. We talk about this stuff all the time. And just because I'm into it one day doesn't mean I'm always up for it. It's my body and I GET TO DECIDE EVERY DANG TIME, just like you do! Veep had no right, MP. I'm so sorry this happened to you and that you felt like you had to go to the question box and not us.

Also, I'm sorry if I said anything that made you feel like a prude. I know you said you don't care and that the word doesn't bother you, but it's still not cool, and it doesn't matter how experienced or conservative or whatever you are, if you don't like the way someone is behaving, that's all that matters.

P.S. I love all you goat mask goddesses! I'm sorry I was being such a cranky, witchy B before. Plz forgive me? xoxo

Forgiven! ← same   Love you
                        xoxo

But that's exactly what I mean. What if it isn't different? Maybe a butt squeeze isn't a big deal and it's me that's overreacting. It's not like I'm an expert when it comes to what's normal at dances. I kept telling myself that it wasn't a big deal, that I was being a prude, but I couldn't stop thinking about it. I can barely look at him. He makes me nervous now. What if he tries to get me alone and do it again? That's why I agreed to skip SL that day. I'm worried that something else might happen.

P.S. You have to swear not to tell anyone! I don't want to talk about it with anyone else yet, I'm so confused. I'm not even sure what I want to happen (other than no more butt squeezing!).

MP, I wish you had told us right away! I hate that you've been worried about this for a week and you never said anything! We could have helped so much earlier. You cannot just squeeze someone's butt without asking. It's not "what everyone is doing now," and even if some people were, you don't want his hands on your butt and

that's enough. You have to go to Coach.
I'll go with you if you want. I'm so mad on
your behalf right now!

And say what? He squeezed my butt at
a dance? Writing it out makes me feel so
stupid. It's not that serious. It didn't hurt, it
didn't even leave a mark, although I could still
feel it for a long time after. But it's not like
it's rape.

Let's say I do tell someone, what if they
don't believe me? I know people saw us
dancing — Twix, you even took a picture of
us — but nobody saw anything. What if I work
up the nerve to tell someone and then he
says it didn't happen? How am I supposed to
prove it? Sunny, you said it yourself, it would
be worse to put it all out there only to have
no one believe me.

I get it, MP, I would feel the same way.
Like what are they going to do over a
butt squeeze, suspend him? He'd come
back to school eventually and then what?

You'd still see him at SL. It's on you to find a way to make things normal, which really sucks. I wish I knew what to say. I want to help!

It's driving me crazy, I can't focus on class or even SL, which is something I actually like and really wanted to do! The day I was supposed to tutor you, Sunny, he followed me into the Student Leadership office and I was so scared he was trying to get me alone that I just bolted before he could say much and went straight home. I forgot all about our study date and just panicked. All I could think about was what if he tried to touch me again? What would I do?

Okay, this is serious. It's taking over your life! We have to do something. If you don't want to talk to Coach or an adult, maybe you could call that anonymous line? Maybe they can give you some tips.

Or you could talk to Veep? Tell him that you didn't appreciate him touching you like that. One of us could come with you. Even if he wasn't trying to upset you, he obviously did and he should know that.. If he's a good guy and it was an accident or just him being presumptuous, maybe he'll apologize.

I can barely look at him, let alone talk to him! Maybe that will change, but right now I'd rather not see him at all. Maybe his family will just up and move? What are the chances of that happening?

I liked all the stuff you guys reported from the class on consent. It made me feel less crazy. I like what Coach said about silence not meaning yes. I feel better knowing that it's okay to feel uncomfortable. I'm just not sure what to do yet.

I also feel so much better writing about it here and discussing it with all of you, my dearest Padlings. I wish I had told you sooner, it probably would have saved me a lot of anxiety. Also, did you hear me in French today? I could barely get a word out. My stutter has been so bad this week. It's like everything is falling apart.

☆

Oct 28

☆ Reasons Why MP Is the BEST:
A Starter List

- Smartest person in class, probably the school! Or the whole city?!

- Not at all self-centred.

- Has the kindest heart.

- One of my favourite laughs (so infectious, in a good way)

- Ran for Student Leadership and gave the best speech, even though she is → terrified of public speaking.

And totally Rocked it!

- Really great boobs (srsly don't be mad), which no one should touch

☆

unless they ask first and have
MP's permission!

- Always looks put together and professional in those little baby blazers, even though we are still in middle school.

- Mature and thoughtful.

- Great hair ←THE GREATEST!

- Wants to make school and the world a better place.

- Knows what she wants & is not afraid to go for it.

- Freakishly good at memorizing lyrics!

- Amazing handwriting.

- Cares deeply about things that other people are too busy to notice.

- Considers everyone's feelings and opinions equally.

- So nice to her family.

- Includes everyone in everything.

- Brave xo

- Brave!

- The **ABSOLUTE** bravest!

Oct 29

You guys are the best. I'm going to copy this list and keep it for when I'm feeling bad and need a pick-me-up. I don't know what I'd do without you.

You should definitely copy it down! Actually, why don't you keep the PAD for awhile? Then it's like we're with you all the time. Have you decided what you want to do about Veep?

I know I said this before, but I'm SO sorry this happened to you, MP. And I'm sorry about all the times I teased you about Veep. I had no idea he was a HANDSY JERK. It must have made you feel even worse. Forgive me?

Also, I know there's a lot going on so I will totally understand if you don't want to come to the recital on Saturday.

Are you kidding? Of course I'll be there!
I love watching you play! An afternoon of
soothing classical music is just what my
frazzled nerves need! Plus I don't want to
miss an opportunity to see Violin Boy!

You are TOO SWEET but I would def lower your expectations.

My parents have conscripted me into
candy duty for Halloween, which is fine by
me, actually. I don't really feel like getting
dressed up this year. I don't like the idea
of people looking at me right now, even
if I was in a disguise. Plus I really do like
seeing all the kids in their costumes —
they're so cute! You're all welcome to join
me. We can pick out all the good candy
before the trick-or-treaters show up,
and then watch a movie or something
after.

I haven't made a decision about Veep, but
I'm going to the SL meeting next week, no
more skipping! We'll see how I feel then.

MP, just let us know what you decide and if you need us for back-up or a little harmless threat, we are there (#FallopianForever). I'll definitely be at the recital, only I can't stay too late. I'm going to a Halloween party with Fifteen, so I want to make sure I have enough time to get ready. He's going as some skateboarder I've never heard of. It doesn't sound that much different than what he usually wears, TBH. I guess he's not really into Halloween.

I can't decide between old-timey street urchin (Bachelor #3 has a crazy collection of old man hats and tweed, you have no idea) and Wonder Woman (it's my fun sister's old costume). I'm not sure I have the boobs to pull off the Wonder Woman costume, plus the skirt is shorter than I would normally like, but I feel like I need to step it up, as it's going to be mostly high schoolers. Or maybe they're more like Fifteen and

not into Halloween. I also don't want
to be the nerd who overdressed.
Sunny, is there any way you could
come with me? Hoops, I assume
you have a hot Halloween date with
Swoosh, but you could come too, if
you want. Might be nice to have my
girls with me!

OMG I WISH! I would be so honoured
and totally excited to go with you, but
my parents are making me take my
brother out for Halloween as part of my
punishment for failing the math test. He's
going as Spider-Man. AGAIN. I think this
is the fourth year in a row or something.
Seriously, doesn't he understand that
the point of Halloween is to be something
different every year? What's so fun
about the same old gross totally generic
costume?

I can totally pass for a fifth grader, so
I'll at least get some decent candy out

of this. I guess that's one good thing
about being so flat. My mom got me this
old-fashioned Harlequin clown costume.
I think deep down she feels bad about
ruining my social life. It's actually pretty
cute. It's black and white and sort of
classy, but not sexy or childish or anything.
Plus I'm going to do full makeup. I found
this awesome YouTube tutorial. I'll take
lots of pics!

P.S. Twix, my vote is for old-timey street
urchin. I bet you will totally stand out
and be ADORABLE! Plus a Wonder Woman
Halloween costume is the teenage
equivalent to Spider-Man. TOTALLY basic
and you are NOT basic! OMG if we were
going out together we'd be so cute and
vintage!

P.P.S. Do people really stop dressing up for
Halloween in high school? TRAGIC!

Swoosh is coming over, but we're not going
trick-or-treating or anything like that.
We're just going to watch something scary.

Before you get too excited, it will be in the living room with the lights on and my mother basically five feet away, so not exactly romantic, but it is officially a date, so there's that!

YAH! GET IT, GIRL! That is big news! It's your first official date, right? The group thing at MP's doesn't count and the dance doesn't really, either. You mostly just walked there together. That's more like a prelude to a date. But this is an actual, scheduled, one-on-one date! And a scary movie is perfect. You can pretend to be frightened and cuddle up or grab his hand in a scary part. What are you going to wear?

P.S. Thanks, Sunny — old-timey street urchin it is!

Did you read the part about my mother basically chaperoning from the next room? We never talked about costumes. Do you think I should dress up? I guess I'm one of those people who doesn't like Halloween all that much. (Sorry, Sunny!) I have some cat ears around somewhere. Maybe I'll put those on. Or, MP, do you still have that old cloak? I could go as a wizard, maybe.

YOU CAN'T JUST PUT CAT EARS ON AND CALL IT A COSTUME! Wear something cute! It's your first official date AND Halloween! I don't have anything that would work, but Twix, maybe your sister does? She's kind of tall like Hoops!

Don't worry about it, I'll just borrow something from my mom and be a girl from the 90s or something. It's not a big deal. I don't think Swoosh is into Halloween, either.

Nov 2

Eight weeks til Christmas!

WAY TOO SOON, Sunny

Happy post-Halloween! I brought a bunch of candy. Does anyone like rockets? They taste like powdery vitamins to me, blech. MP, Hoops texted to tell me something about Veep showing up at your house?! How dare he! That's like, stalking! What did you do?

Yeah, it was totally unexpected, but I wouldn't exactly call it stalking. He showed up with this group of football players who came to the door trick-or-treating. They were all wearing helmets so I couldn't see their faces, but I knew they were too old to be trick-or-treating, so I told them I was saving the candy for kids and they could just move along. They complained a little but eventually started to move on, only one of them stayed behind on the step and once the others were out of earshot, he took off his helmet and it was Veep.

I think I might have gasped out loud, I'm not sure. But I swear I could feel all the colour drain from my face and my hands were shaky. But before I could shut the door, he asked me to please wait. That's exactly what he said, "Please wait." Something about that "please" calmed me down a bit, so I said "What for?" and he asked if I was mad at him.

I didn't trust myself to say anything, so I just shrugged. I was shaking so hard I had to hold my elbows. He said that he heard about That Question and he'd been thinking about it all week and then he asked if I put the question in the box.

I asked him why he thought that, and then he blushed and he said he was thinking about how after we danced, I just walked away and haven't spoken to him since.

"It feels like you're avoiding me. I know you skipped Student Leadership, because Danika saw you in the lunchroom that day. Then you ran away from me after school. It's almost like you're scared of me."

He looked nervous, and a little confused, and suddenly I wasn't so scared anymore. "You really freaked me out," I said. "You can't just touch people like that." He got really nervous, and said, "I didn't mean to freak you out. I really like you. It wasn't, like, harassment." And I said, "Well, it felt like that to me." We talked a bit longer . . . and that's when the shouting started and these two pirates came running toward us.

P.S. Do you have any mini chocolate bars? My brother ate all the good ones.

Okay, but think of it from my perspective! There I was, sitting on the couch with Swoosh, pretending to watch a horror movie and not think about his leg touching mine or my mother who was "reading" in the next room, and I just happened to look up and I see Veep cornering MP in the doorway! At least that's what it looked like to me. I stood up so fast the popcorn went everywhere and my mom came running in to see what happened, but I just ran for the door and started yelling! I never really thought about what it would look like to you or Veep.

P.S. Our conversation about costumes got me worried that maybe Swoosh was into Halloween and so my mom and I found enough bits and pieces around the house to turn me into a pirate. I wore one of her old white shirts over tights and a red sash plus an eye-patch and those boots that look like they belong to Robin Hood. Or a pirate, I guess.

P.P.S. Swoosh's costume was way better. He was some pirate from a video game I've never heard of. And before you say anything about how cute it was that we both dressed as pirates, I KNOW! My mom only said it a hundred times. Then she insisted on taking all these photos of us and starting talking like an actual pirate. Like, "Arrrrrrren't you two cute?" I thought I was going to die of embarrassment. Swoosh just kind of laughed and I told her she was under no circumstances allowed to post them.

OMG I wish I was there to see you and your Pirate King charge across the lawn! TAKE THAT, SL SCUM! Do not anger the Goddess of Basketball! What did Veep do? This is waaay more exciting than my Halloween, BTW. More on that later, I need to find out what happens!

P.S. Sunny, do you have anything sour in your bag-o-treats? I will gladly accept any sour candy in the form of kids, keys, cherries or gumballs.

Swoosh was right there behind her. They both came tearing out of the house at full speed. Hoops was the only one yelling, though. Swoosh looked a little concerned, but mostly confused. At first I thought there as an emergency, like a fire or something. I asked Hoops what the matter was, and she said, "What's going on? What is he doing here?"

Veep looked terrified, like they were going to attack him right there on the front step. He actually held his football helmet in front of him like it was a shield!

"I just came to apologize," Veep said.
"Well, go on!" Hoops said. (BTW Hoops, you TOTALLY sounded like your mom there, but in a good way!)

← UM, WE'RE FIGHTING NOW jk

And then he turned back to me, said he was sorry, and he hoped that he would see me at SL next week. So I said he would, and then he turned to leave, but Hoops wasn't moving so he had to kind of squeeze between her and Swoosh. It was kind of amazing.

I THINK YOU MEAN TOTALLY AMAZING! Hoops, you are MY QUEEN! And Swoosh came too! That's so sweet! And I love that you both dressed as pirates — that's some crazy Love-Magic at work! You were obviously meant to be together. (We can say that now, right? It's official?) You're

like awesome squared. Or doubled?
Whatever, you are Awesome to the
power of WICKED!

I can't believe Veep just showed up
at your door out of nowhere! It's
good he apologized, though. How do
you feel about things, MP? Are you
still thinking about going to a teacher
about the butt squeeze? Or Coach?

No, he genuinely felt bad and he didn't realize
how upset I was about everything. He looked
really shaken, even before Hoops came
crashing across the yard dressed like a pirate.
Plus I did tell someone, I told all of you. And I
guess Swoosh knows now too? That's kind of
awkward.

Hoops, I know you want me to tell Coach, but
I don't want to get him in trouble. I think
he really, truly feels badly about it. And I
know for sure now that I'm not crazy or
overreacting, that what he did was over the
line. I doubt he'll do anything like that again.

He's not a bad guy, he just didn't know he was
doing anything wrong. He definitely does now.
That's enough for me.

It's your decision, MP. If you are satisfied
with how things ended, then I will be too.
He did look sort of queasy, which was
satisfying in its own way.

And BTW, Swoosh doesn't know anything
about it. I told him it was girl stuff and
he didn't ask any other questions. But if
he did know, I think he's the kind of guy
who can keep a secret.

P.S. Enough with the love pirate stuff.
Twix, how was your party?

Obviously nothing could possibly
be as major as MP getting the
acknowledgement and closure she
deserves. SRSLY, I think the fact that
he came to talk to you is a good sign
that he's not a horrible, evil person.

I'm still not Team Veep, but I take back my "SL scum" comment. Plus how lucky are you to have badass Hoops next door to rush to your aid?

Honestly, the party was just okay. There were way more people at this one. It was so crowded and loud and most of them were just trying to hook up with each other. People were like, polite, but mostly they ignored me and spent the whole night laughing about these inside jokes I obviously didn't get. Fifteen barely talked to me, and when I said I wasn't having a good time, he said it was cool if I wanted to leave, but he was going to stay, and then he went and talked to this totally beautiful girl dressed like some anime character I've never heard of, so I just left. He hasn't texted me since. I'm kind of bummed, but it's not like I'm in love with him or anything. We don't have the LOVE-MAGIC, as Sunny would say. It's not like we spontaneously decided to dress as pirates without talking to each other first like SOME PEOPLE. 😜

Plus, okay now don't get mad, but I can't stop thinking about Dimples and that moment we had at the dance. He's texted a few times since and I think there's still something there. Maybe the very early beginnings of Love-Magic? I'd like to see where it goes, at least. If MP can give Veep a second chance, then surely I can give Dimples one.

P.S. Sunny you were so right, there were three different Wonder Women there.

Nov 3

So, are we just not going to talk about how Violin Boy gave Sunny FLOWERS at the recital?

OK GOOD I AM DYING TO TALK ABOUT IT, but obviously I want to make sure MP is okay. Plus I know I texted you all a million pictures, but I'm just so excited! Honestly, the whole thing feels like a dream except I have a vase of flowers on my dresser to prove it actually happened! Well, it's not really a vase, it's an old pickle jar, but I wrapped some strips of cute Washi tape around it and it looks so pretty and rustic and contains FLOWERS FROM AN ACTUAL BOY!

BEAUTIFUL!

Insta worthy!

Looks store-bought!

Srsly I've been floating since Saturday, even trick-or-treating with the monster and his two equally monster friends (THAT'S RIGHT, THE TRIO OF TERROR) was bearable! Anything is bearable when you've received your first bouquet of flowers! I thought my mom would lose it if she saw a boy giving me a gift, but I think even she was impressed. It helps that he's basically a prodigy. When he walked away all she said was, "He seems like a nice boy." PROGRESS!!

I texted him on Sunday to say thank you and he sent a thumbs up, which isn't the most romantic response, but I think MP was right, he's totally shy, so I'm going to take things really slow. EEEEEEEE!!!

P.S. Twix, I'm sorry about Fifteen, but he was too old and boring for you anyway. How could any straight boy in his right mind choose to skateboard with his bros when you are right there being awesome and beautiful? It's his loss! And I'm in such a good, floaty mood that I'm going to forget all about Dimples ditching you at the movies and his questionable friends, and say go for it!

So much Love-Magic in the air! Seriously, I'm much better now, and I'm so happy for you, Sunny! I knew he liked you, he's just shy! After the recital, he was standing by the water fountain by himself but he kept looking over at us. I could tell he was nervous because the flowers in his hands were shaking. I had a feeling they were for you, and that's why I pulled Twix and Hoops away to the refreshment table.

MP, you brilliant schemer! I wish I didn't have my back to the whole thing, but I was very distracted by

the junk bars (SRly, WHAT is in those?!
ARe you suRe it's legal?) and all the
otheR amazing RefRreshments on
display. What did he say exactly? I
want to know eveRy woRd.

So I admit, at first I was like, why are
my friends ditching me all of a sudden,
but then I saw Violin Boy coming toward
me and before I could get nervous he
was right there shoving the flowers in my
face. Here's our exact convo:

Violin Boy: Hi. I thought your sonatina
  was really good.

Sunny: Thank you! So did you. I mean,
            you were really great, too.

Violin Boy: I brought these for you.
  They're from my garden.

  Sunny: They're so beautiful, thank
  you! And I'm sorry about the cookie
                  thing, I didn't know.

Violin Boy: It's okay, I only had one bite. Did you make the lemon squares over at the refreshment table?

Sunny: Yes, and the junk bars and the snickerdoodles. I'm really into baking.

Violin Boy: My dad's had two already. He said they were the best lemon squares he's ever had.

 Sunny: Maybe I could try a gluten-free recipe. I really want to be a more inclusive baker.

Violin Boy: Cool. I mean, if you want to. See you at theory.

Sunny: See you!

So now, I have to try some amazing gluten-free recipes. Hoops, does your mom have any that she really likes? Maybe something with ginger?

P.S. I googled the flowers and found out  that Chrysanthemums symbolize love, friendship and joy. LOVE, FRIENDSHIP AND JOY!!!! It's a sign!

And to think, a few weeks ago you weren't even going to talk to him! See what happens when you take matters into your own hands? My mom doesn't really bake much, but I can ask her about gluten-free recipes.

P.S. Did you really say you wanted to be an "inclusive baker?"

OMG yes, it just sort of popped out of my mouth! I hope it didn't sound too weird. It's not NOT true! I definitely don't want to kill people with my baking! Especially very cute people who bring me flowers of LOVE, FRIENDSHIP AND JOY!!

Nov 4

Last day of sex ed! So sad, I'm really going to miss the question box. Today someone wanted to know if you could get a sexually transmitted infection from

kissing. Answer: Most STIs are spread
through genital contact or by exchanging
bodily fluids (gross), but it is possible to
get herpes from kissing someone with the
herpes virus, so you should avoid kissing
people with open sores around their mouth,
which, no problem (cringe)!

Actually, there are two kinds of herpes virus.
One is the kind that usually causes cold sores
on your mouth. The other one is usually
sexually transmitted and it can cause lesions
in the genital area.

I'm sorry, Coach? Is that you? How do you
know so much about herpes, MP?

Because I get cold sores! Not from kissing,
obviously, but you can get them from other
things too. It's a pretty common virus. The
first time I had a cold sore, I went to the
doctor and she told me about the two kinds
of herpes virus. I looked it up during one of

my so-called "free periods" in the library
when I was doing my handwashing research
for Mr. M. Looks like the sex ed student has
now become the teacher! Who knew?!

Okay, confession, that was my
question. (Swoosh was right, I
did put something in.) I'm sure
you guys have noticed the giant
weeping THING on my upper lip
and have just been too nice to say
anything about it. It appeared
after I started seeing Fifteen and
My Fun Sister made a comment
about kissing and herpes and I
kind of panicked, so I put that
question in the box.

Turns out it's not even herpes,
it is the king of zombie zits. I
swear, there is like a family of
them growing in that one spot.

Anyway, I was too embarrassed to tell all of you, which is dumb, I know. From now on I promise I will share my deepest, darkest and grossest thoughts with you (don't say I didn't warn you). 😉

Um, glad to hear you don't have herpes, Twix, but more importantly, I have super secret, life-changing

BREAKING NEWS!
The Little Red Engine has pulled into town! I REPEAT
THE LITTLE RED ENGINE HAS PULLED INTO TOWN!

SUNNY, NO WAY!!!!! You got your period?!?

Oh hurray! I know how much you wanted this, Sunny. What happened? Are you feeling okay? Do you need a pad or anything?

It was me, I got my period. Seriously, Sunny, you didn't have to make it so confusing! Also what did I tell you about calling it the Little Red Train? It's just a period, don't try and make it cutesy.

I was in the bathroom stall at lunch and like, there it was. I had zero warning. No cramps, no nothing. For a minute I was, like, what am I looking at? It's not as red as I thought it would be. It looked more like a smear, almost like a skid mark? Shudder! But then I was like, that's not possible, so I guess this is it. My period. Kind of a let-down, really.

LOL I TOTALLY know what you mean about it looking like a skid mark. Nobody tells you that part! I was expecting a gushing, bright red river that would be impossible to control, but mine was more brownish and pretty light the first time. Now my period is a little longer and there's more blood. The colour changes a bit each day, too. You get used to it. Hurray, Hoops! Welcome to the menstruator's club!

Don't say club, I already feel left out. Of course I'm the last one to get it. But today is not about me. Today is about Hoops and where she wants to go to celebrate!

I can't believe you got it at school! That was one of my biggest fears. I was so relieved when I got mine at home over the summer. At least I was in my own house and could deal with everything in private. You're lucky that Sunny was there!

I know! I totally owe you, Sunny. I had a just-in-case pad in my backpack, but it was in my locker so Sunny went and brought it to me, no big deal. I can't wait to get home and change into my period underwear.

This pad feels a bit like a diaper. But while I was sitting there on the toilet, it made made me think about what your Fun Sister said about pads and tampons being available for free in bathrooms, Twix. I didn't have any change on me. I never bring money to school. Plus they should find a way to put them in the stalls. It's not like I'm about to waddle out, bleeding, in front of anyone who might come in.

I have had this exact same thought, but maybe there is something we can do about it. I read your Fun Sister's article, Twix, and she mentioned programs and websites that have resources on menstruation equity. I looked them up when I was in the library and there are so many ideas for drives and fundraising. Maybe we could have a menstrual product drive here at school, just like the food drive. I could bring it up at the student leadership meeting next week.

P.S. Did you know that in Scotland they passed a bill that made period products free to those who need them?

BRB MOVING TO SCOTLAND!

SO cool!

I love this idea, but MP I know you hate talking about private stuff, are you sure you want to? Maybe we can all come to the meeting for moral support?

Honestly this makes so much sense!

Honestly, we've been talking about this stuff in the PAD so much that I feel better about it now. It feels kind of normal. Oops, I forgot we're trying not to use that word! Not normal, ordinary. Having a period feels like an ordinary, everyday thing to me now. If everyone talked about it more, then it wouldn't be a big deal at all. Like Twix's favourite poster said, Be the change you want to see!

HAHA!

But yes, I'd love all my Padlings to be there!

I LOVE this idea! I will come to
the meeting and make signs and
recite Fallopian Forever, whatever
you need, MP! You're my hero, the
real-life Menstruator, changing
the world, one bathroom stall
at a time! We have so much to
celebrate. Where are we going?
It should be your choice, Hoops,
since it's your first period. I know
we talked about DQ, but it could
be literally anywhere. I wanna
talk about MP's rad idea, but also
we can help you figure out how
you're going to handle your mom.
She's going to totally flip. We
should go right after school. There
isn't any basketball or student
Leadership or anything, right?

P.S. Now we HAVE to make those
Sisterhood of the Goat Mask
t-shirts! Or maybe Menstruators
of the Goat Mask??

No, thank God. I really don't feel like running around. My stomach feels kind of heavy. Maybe this is the beginning of cramps? It doesn't feel like a cramp, exactly. Not at all what you have to deal with, MP. Plus I'm worried about the smell. Can you smell it? Be honest!

As a person who is sitting right behind you, I swear I cannot smell anything but the usual horrible classroom smells. Do they even clean this room? Ugh! You know what smells really nice? MY FLOWERS! THE ONES I GOT FROM VIOLIN BOY! ☺

I'm free after school too! Do you want to go to that Portuguese bakery by my house? They have those amazing gooey egg tarts that are super yum. I wish I could make them but they are too advanced for me.

But wherever you want to go, Hoops, it's your period we're celebrating!

We can also just go to Starbucks on the corner, it's close and has lots of choices. Maybe you should get those red velvet cake things. You know, RED velvet, because of your RED period?

Twix, please don't associate a beloved dessert with the colour of my bodily fluids. Plus if that was the case, it would be a brown dessert, like the banana chocolate chip bread.

Your period is the colour of banana bread? That's gross, but also how come they always make it sound like it's going to be this bright red colour?

I told you, Sunny, the colour changes! Everything changes. That's my bit of wisdom for the day. Now. Hoops, WYR eat gooey egg tarts or period red velvet cake?

Since you put it like that, neither. And since it's my period we are celebrating, I don't have to observe regular WYR rules. I want ice cream, like we talked about originally.

I was hoping you were going to say ice cream! I'm in. I can't wait. "Happee 1st Period Dae, Hoops!" (Get it?)

Yes, I got it. Thanks a lot, HAGRID. Please don't put that on an ice cream cake.

P.S. Do you think the bathrooms at Hogwarts have dispensers or do you think there's a conjuring spell?

Do you think Wonder Woman gets a period? Or Eleven from Stranger Things?

Maybe that's why Eleven is so powerful! She IS The Menstruator!

I still can't believe you watch Stranger Things, it's way too scary for me. But it makes you think, why does no one ever get a period in shows or movies? I seriously can't think of any right now!

Me neither. Okay, witch periods aside (NERDS!), imagine if we did get something written on the cake though? And some dude in the back has to spell out "Congrats on starting your period" in icing? That would be kind of amazing.

I LOVE the idea of period cakes! If everyone got period cakes maybe people would be less weirded out by periods. Think of how many times people would be buying them! It would become totally normal. Like birthday cakes, but twelve times a year, times half the population! I don't know the exact number of cakes that would be, but I do know it's a LOT! OMG . . . maybe I should open a period cake bakery?!

I am on board with normalizing periods and Sunny opening a bakery dedicated to period cakes, but I don't want cake. I just want one of those mudslide things, so maybe we can save the cake decorating idea for Sunny's period party?

You mean you DON'T want "Expecto Menstronus" piped in red icing on an ice cream cake?

I do! And I don't even like HP!

I would totally do that! Forget the mochaccino, I want a cookies and crème ice cream cake but I'm going with the old school Fallopian 4ever written in chocolate icing. HURRY UP, PERIOD HORMONES! Yay! It's been a long time since we did something all together outside of school.

Okay great! I'm so pumped I kinda want to cut out now! Don't worry, I know none of you would never, ever do something as scandalous as skip class, but if there was ever a reason to skip class, this is it! Period cakes are just the beginning! On the first day of your period you shouldn't have to go to school. It should be a day of rest and pampering and respect for the TOTAL MAGIC of the female body #FallopianForever

* SAME!

I am on board with this #FallopianForever

Me, too, but not the skipping class part. #FallopianForever

Can you believe the PAD is almost full? I thought it would be this fun thing we did for a little while, but now I don't want to stop! There's a dollar store right by the DQ, we can pick out PAD 2.0 together after Hoops' Period Party. I'M SO EXCITED!

P.S. FALLOPIAN FOREVER!!!!

WE, THE SISTERHOOD OF THE GOAT MASK,

UNDERSTAND THE POWER OF WORDS AND THEREFORE WE STRIKE THESE OFFENSIVE WORDS AND PHRASES FROM OUR VOCABULARY:

- Normal
- Prude
- Slut
- The Big Red Train
- The Big Red Dog
- Aunt Flo

WE SOLEMNLY SWEAR TO USE THE
FOLLOWING WORDS ONCE A WEEK
WHEN IT IS APPROPRIATE: ↰ I did not
agree to this

Same!

Fixed!

- Period
- Vulva
- Vagina
- Masturbation
- Heteronormative
- Menstruator
- Fallopian

Acknowledgements

I am so grateful to my real-life Sisterhood of the Goat Mask, aka the many people who've touched P.S. Tell No One in some way. Special thanks to editor Anne Shone, who was an early champion of this book and gently let me know when my age was showing (shudder!). I've always imagined this book taking the form of a diary, and designer Yvonne Lam made my dreams come true and then some. Yvonne's design choices elevate the reading experience and help make the characters feel like real people. Holly Allerellie's art brings so much humour and personality to the book, and I will never see a cuter rendition of the female reproductive system. Thank you to everyone at Scholastic Canada, especially Diane Kerner, Sabrina Mirza, Erica Fyvie, Jenn Hubbs, Nikole Kritikos and Gui Fillipone. Thanks to my friends and family who have listened to me rant about periods and menstrual equity at any given opportunity.

Look, I finally put my pen where my mouth is! Lastly, when I was in grade six, my friends and I kept a pass-around diary, which was the inspiration for this book. I am grateful to Shannon, Gillian, Sarah and Katie for being my friends, and for Mrs. Tonner, who caught us in the act but instead of punishing us, encouraged us to keep writing. #FallopianForever

Vikki VanSickle is an award-winning author and a devoted member of the Canadian children's book industry. She began her career as a bookseller and went on to spend twelve years in publishing, focused on marketing children's books. Frequently referred to as "Canada's Judy Blume," Vikki is the author of a number of acclaimed books, including three picture books, and the novels *Words that Start with B*, *Summer Days, Starry Nights* and the 2018 Red Maple Award winner *The Winnowing*. Vikki speaks about kids' books as CTV *Your Morning*'s resident bookworm. And she is the Education Coordinator at the Period Purse, a non-profit that focuses on menstrual equity and ending the stigma around menstruation. Originally from Woodstock, Vikki now lives in Toronto with her cat.